THE TIES THAT DIVIDE

SANDRA & TAYLOR PREISLER

Copyright © 2024 by Taylor & Sandra Preisler

ISBN (ebook): 979-8-9900489-3-5
ISBN (Paperback): 979-8-9900489-0-4
ISBN (Hardcover): 979-8-9900489-1-1
ISBN (Large Print): 979-8-9900489-4-2

All rights reserved.

No part of this book may be reproduced in any form or by any electronic or mechanical means, including information storage and retrieval systems, without written permission from the author, except for the use of brief quotations in a book review.

Title Production by The BookWhisperer

Cover design by Sandy Robson

To Wilma, AKA Chilly Willy. You were the coolest mom and grandma around. You laughed out loud at life, turned getting lost in a book into an art form, and handed down a love of reading as a legacy. Unfailingly, you believed in us. Without you, there would be no book. You are still missed.

Chapter One

"You let her run wild."

It was a statement, not a question. Hugh Dovefield sighed and looked at his wife, Simone, before answering—in this case, before not answering. He did consider a counter argument, but was held back by the rather obvious fact that she was right. He gazed out the window of his Hyde Street home and watched as his stepdaughter, Zoe, ran the last few yards to his front door, followed with reluctance by her lady's maid. Her laughter rang out as she entered the dining room, her bright blue eyes alight and her dark mass of turbulent curls tumbling downward as she removed her bonnet.

She spoke without preamble. "Hyde Park at dawn is an absolute marvel. The sun touches the tops of the trees like the kiss of the gods."

With the dramatic flair of an artist, she collapsed with less than ladylike grace into a chair and immediately demanded coffee. The room stilled as Zoe reached for the milk, having finally taken in her surroundings.

"I didn't realize you would be up at this hour, *mama*." She said it the French way, with the accent on the end.

"There are many things you fail to realize." Simone smoothed her robe as she rose and walked gracefully to the table. As always, she radiated dignity and control, even in her voice. She paused, demonstrating her own flair for the dramatic. "Like how many gentlemen will want a wife who escapes at dawn to paint the light of sunrise."

"Fortunately, I am in no need of a gentleman." Zoe met her mother's eyes squarely as she raised her cup to drink. "So, we may never know."

Even in this informal state, with her hair still braided from the night and her dressing gown open and flowing, there was no missing the steel in Simone's eyes as she spoke in a low voice. *"Il faut jouer le jeu pour gagner."*

Zoe lowered her eyes as a flush colored her cheeks. *One must play the game to win.* Her mother had won the game she played. Only Zoe knew how much she first lost. She raised her eyes to see her mother gliding around the table to her side.

"You will remain inside for the day, Zoe." Some found Simone's slight French accent charming, but to Zoe it was as hard as steel. "No more running about. We will receive callers after our noon meal, and tonight you can remain with the family. Perhaps, somehow, you could attempt to act like a lady." Simone turned to leave, but at the door she paused for a final biting word. "At the very least, look like one tonight."

Zoe was silent for a moment. Simone's presence seemed to fill the room even when her physical self was absent. Not for the first time, she wondered how such a petite woman could command such space.

"She means well," murmured Hugh. "Never forget that."

"You think that because love has blinded you."

He chuckled. "People our age aren't blinded by the whirlwind of love the way young people are—the way you will be."

Zoe made a face. "We shall see. Tell me the story of how you and mama met."

"You must've heard that story a hundred times. You should know it by heart by now."

"Tell me anyway." Zoe put her elbows on the table and leaned forward, her chin resting in her upturned palms. "Seeing her through your eyes reminds me she's human."

"Very well." Hugh sighed, but there was a smile behind his long suffering facade. "As you know, I was married in my youth, but my first wife died young and so I was a widower for many years. I simply was not interested in marrying again. I had my work as a barrister, and I was wholly dedicated to that. I was approaching my mid-forties, thinking quite happily that was all my life would be. But—"

"Fate had other plans," said Zoe with a grin.

"Indeed. One day I arrived early for dinner at my older brother's London home when his children's new French tutor walked by. She was a petite creature, with long blonde hair and those piercing blue eyes.

From the moment I saw her, she was the very definition of beauty to me, and when her eyes met mine...it was as if the floor had dropped out from under my feet."

"Blinded by love, just like I said."

Hugh shook his head with a smile. "I was taken with her from the start, I'll say that. But I was never blind as to who your mother was. I saw the thorns as well as the rose."

"Hmm. Was I a part of the rose, or a thorn?"

He patted her arm. "You were a blessing, and still are. I remember you too on that day—nine years old, just a slip of a girl, hiding behind your mother's skirt. If looks could kill... you sized me up like a cat with a mouse, with absolute menace in your eyes. I liked you immediately."

"The feeling was not mutual." Zoe laughed. "It wasn't personal though. I was a very angry child."

"You had reason to be. And it all worked out in the end. I know you know this, but just remember that everything your mother did, she did for you. She loves you Zoe, and she always means well, even when her words are sharp."

A servant came in with a fresh pot of coffee, and Zoe took a moment to refill both her cup and his. The love of the bitter beverage was another thing the duo had in common.

"I do know. Truth be told, Lucy is far more aggravating than *mama* at this point." She took another sip of coffee and continued. "She is so very dire. Getting her to go with me this morning was more work than the walk. She is quite convinced we will be killed by rogues, as if Hyde Park is filled with bandits."

Hugh's expression turned into a frown as he cleared his throat. "She is a bit retiring, to be sure. Good maids are difficult to procure. She is competent and loyal, and those are the important qualities."

Zoe snorted in a most unladylike fashion and tossed her dark curls over her shoulder in a dramatic fashion. "She is a bore, Father. A simple bore. Perhaps we should look for another—someone more cheerful and less melancholic."

"We don't trade in people because they bore us, Zoe." Most of the time her stepfather let her have her own way, but when his voice took that edge and his eyes hardened, Zoe knew the conversation was over.

She sighed, but didn't push the subject. Hugh Dovefield was known far and wide for his liberal humanitarian views. He lived what he preached, often defending the downtrodden in court, even those who could not pay. His belief that every person had a right to a defense won both friends and enemies. His steadfast loyalty to his French wife and her daughter, on the other hand, won him both women's respect.

Zoe remembered those early times, sipping her brew while becoming thoughtful. It had been difficult at first, when he wed her mother. She was angry, hostile even, after the loss of both her father and her home. They had been part of the Great Exodus, when the nobles of France ran for their very lives from their homeland, and the streets ran with their very blood. It was only through Simone's resourcefulness and intelligence that she and Zoe had arrived alive on British shores. Zoe's father was not so lucky.

The two years that followed were years of poverty and hunger, as the little money they'd been able to bring ran low and Simone was forced to work for their survival. Even Hugh didn't know their story in its entirety. But Simone's beauty and her impeccable manners finally earned her steady employment as a French tutor. She was able to feed and clothe the two of them, but life was never easy, and the constant stress took its toll.

When the wedding took place, Zoe sulked the entire day, refusing to speak to either her mother or Hugh. It was one more change in her young life over which she had no control. She managed to keep up that dislike for a while, well past when most men would have tolerated such an attitude.

It was the nightmares that changed things, thought Zoe.

As Zoe rose to leave, Hugh spoke his parting wisdom. "Do try to get along with your mother today. It's not the end of the world to stay in for a day."

Looking back at her stepfather, she paused at the door. "I will do my best, Father. But you know *mama* and I..."

Her voice trailed off as she left, but she knew Hugh understood the meaning.

Zoe bounded up the stairs two at a time. Her mother could rest easy for a while as she wanted to finish the drawings that she had sketched that morning, anyway. Reaching her spacious bedroom, she set herself up at the easel and paints near her window and pulled her drawings from her pelisse.

People often commented with surprise at Zoe's talent as an artist. She had learned from those years wandering the streets to be attentive to detail, to pay attention to her surroundings. She could still draw her old address from memory; a place of refuge compared to the months before.

When he saw her natural talent, Hugh engaged an excellent tutor to refine it. She still found joy in bringing her vision to life on paper, both with pencil and paint.

Carefully placing her favorite sketch from the morning in place, she began to add the golds and oranges, bringing the sunrise to life. As the vision took place on the canvas, her thoughts drifted to the real problem at hand —Lucy.

As a maid she was passable, though she did struggle with Zoe's rebellious curls. But the real problem was she lacked any sense of adventure at all, reluctant to even leave the house alone with Zoe. Though she was similar in age, she seemed to fear life as if she were old. She would tiresomely speak of men who could accost them, accidents that could befall them, and illnesses that could overcome them. She preferred to stay inside, serving tea and mending hems. This made her a poor match for her mistress, as much time in the house threatened to suffocate Zoe.

As a child in France, she remembered playing with her father for hours in the sunshine, chasing each other around the trees on their grand estate. She remembered his laughter, and the smell of fresh cut grass, and the soft feel of his hands as he threw her in the air and she gleefully screamed. The progression of time had blurred those early memories, but she still somehow felt closer to him when she was outside.

Later, after fleeing France, she and her mother lived in a tiny flat on the east side. Still, she found solace outside. Her mother would leave each morning, searching for work or for food, and she would follow soon afterwards to wander the streets. Though the foul London air could not compare to the fresh

French countryside, it seemed to fill not only her lungs but her soul to breathe outside.

Which led to the conundrum she was currently facing. A maid who shackled her. She was so engrossed in her work and her thoughts that she did not hear the very subject of those thoughts approach, gasping and jumping when Lucy spoke.

"Milady, Mistress Simone would like to speak with you."

Taking a deep breath, Zoe slowed her beating heart. She didn't have a good grasp on how much time had passed; she rarely did when she was painting.

"Is it time for luncheon?" she asked Lucy.

"It is near, milady, but Mistress Simone would like to speak with you before luncheon." Lucy, her brown hair pulled back in a severe bun, looked uncomfortable.

Zoe sighed. She could only imagine what else her mother wanted to pick a fight about today.

"If you'll remember, milady, it's my half day today. I shall be leaving soon."

"Today? It's Thursday. Your half day is Saturday,"

"If you'll remember, I asked last week to

change that for this week. Mrs. Baring said it would fit well with the servants schedules, so it was allowed."

"Yes, of course. We did speak." Zoe paused. "It's Thursday! I promised Aunt Theo I would be by at tea time to pick up the flier for the next Bluestocking conversation."

Theo, or Theodosia, was Hugh's older sister, and her home was often a meeting place for the men and especially ladies of intellect who gathered for tea and talk.

"And *Mama* is put out. She will never allow my leave." Zoe's darting eyes landed on Lucy. "But you are going out."

The words hung in the air. Expectation remained as they fell.

"I have my own business, milady." Lucy's speech was always impeccable. "I have an appointment I cannot miss."

Zoe's blue eyes hardened. She rarely gave up when her mind was set. "Lucy, its only to Aunt Thea's home. Surely you can fit that in. I will even pay for a hackney to quicken the trip. I need the flier in a timely fashion to pass on to the Ramsbury girls at tomorrow's soiree. Really, I insist."

"I'm sorry, milady, but I cannot do it today."

Zoe's nostrils flared with anger. Why did Lucy have to make everything so much harder than necessary?

"Lucy, I may have given you the impression that I was asking for a favor. You will follow my instructions, or I will speak with Mrs. Baring and tell her your appointment is you sneaking off to meet a man. Then you shall have no half day at all and we shall both be greatly disappointed."

Lucy's face paled. Zoe knew she had crossed a line, but it was too late to back down now.

"Very well, milady, since you insist. But I won't be able to bring the flier home until late this evening."

Zoe smiled. She knew how to get her way. "Thank you, Lucy, that will work. Hand me my reticule."

Chapter Two

"But where could she possibly be?" It wasn't the first time Zoe had asked the question. "She always comes home at night after her half day."

Hugh and Simone continued eating the excellent meal and made no comment. Even in her distracted state, Zoe appreciated that for all her mother's efforts to fit into the English way, she drew the line at English food. Their French cook did a marvelous roast duck. Zoe glanced at her younger siblings. They both must have agreed as they were quite wholly involved in eating.

Shortly after their marriage, Simone produced her first child with her new husband.

Walter, now aged thirteen, was constantly famished, and particularly fond of duck. Despite his appetite, he was still slender, not yet adopting the stocky build of his father.

Three years after Walter's birth, Phoebe arrived. She shared her mother's slight frame, along with her fair hair and blue eyes. At ten years old she was more difficult to please with food, sometimes picking at her meal more than eating. Tonight though, she was attacking the potatoes with ravenous enthusiasm.

Though they were still quite young, both children were well behaved and for the most part even tempered, unlike their older half sister. They looked up as the pause in conversation lengthened, but refrained from comment.

Unfortunately for her mother, that wasn't an option for her. She shared a knowing glance with her husband before addressing Zoe. "It is indeed a mystery where Lucy could be, but not nearly the mystery you seem to have made it out to be in your head. We have been over this. Maids leave all the time, Zoe. You did not even like her, and requested we replace her with regularity. The most likely answer is she simply ran off with a man. We will place an advertisement for a new maid tomorrow. In the meantime, you must stop obsessing about this."

Zoe said nothing, but she knew her parents were wrong. Lucy was plain, old for her age, and just, well...dull. Zoe was positive she did not have a beau in her life, despite yesterday's threat. But she herself could come up with nothing else that could have happened. She just knew it was not a romance. Hence the continued questions.

Lucy had left for her half day with Zoe's words reminding her to go to Theo's. She simply had not returned. Mrs. Baring had noted her absence and questioned the other female servants under her supervision before informing the family, but no one knew what she customarily did on her days off. In truth, none of them knew very much about her at all. When all was said and done, it was as if she'd hardly even existed.

Mature enough to be ashamed of her demands with Lucy, Zoe had told no one of it. Though the troublesome thought had crossed her mind, she thought it extremely unlikely that Lucy would run off after a single harsh exchange with her mistress. A servant needed references to acquire gainful employment, and Lucy wasn't the type to take an action so rash as to abandon her position with no notice. Nonetheless, the timing made Zoe uncomfortable, and the intrusive thought that this was all her fault had wormed its way deep into her brain.

Hugh retired to his study after dining to review a pending case and Simone withdrew to help the children ready themselves for bed. She did not pursue the English way of raising children, allowing nannies, governesses and tutors to bear the bulk of the responsibilities. Of course they had tutors and a governess, but Simone made sure the children were a part of their daily lives, and she always spent the hour before bed with them. Hugh would meet her later in her sitting room to share their customary evening nightcap.

Hugh spent many an evening in preparation for court. He had established himself as a successful and profitable barrister, due to his meticulous research and attention to detail. Many barristers, nearly all of whom were gentlemen who turned their noses up at the mere notion of *earning* a salary, were content to let their solicitors do the bulk of the work. Then they simply went through the motions in court and collected their gratuity. Hugh, on the other hand, was a work horse. He put that effort in for all his clients, regardless of class, whether guilty or innocent, or whether he represented the prosecution or the defense.

When Zoe was young, after she had accepted Hugh as a part of her family, she spent many hours in his study, loving the rich mahogany panels and the masculine woodsy smell that seemed as much a part of the room as the furniture. Hugh's first short marriage had not resulted in any children, and he was delighted from the start to have a daughter in his life, and even better, one who took an interest in his work. Aware of her sharp intelligence, and uninterested in the usual notions of what comprises an appropriate education for a wealthy noble girl, Hugh cheerfully taught her the rules of court and the ins and outs of British law. In her early teens, the two of them had even sneaked Zoe into the courtroom on occasion, unbeknownst to Simone.

Zoe had listened, enthralled as Hugh defended clients, using his nuanced knowledge to poke holes in witness testimony or fluster his opponent. A few clients were of the nobility, and many came from the more modest middle class, and these paid well for his services. But he also represented poor folk, who could pay with little more than gratitude. Even his worst critics couldn't deny Hugh Dovefield was an honorable man.

It had been some time since those long afternoons in the study. Time and the realities of the restrictions placed upon noble women had distanced Zoe from Hugh's profession, but when she entered the study now, still troubled by Lucy's disappearance, she was pleased that the woodsy scent remained the same.

"What if something did happen to her?" Zoe asked without preamble. "What if it isn't a man? How would we know?"

"If Lucy were in trouble and needed help, or money, or a reference, she would send word, Zoe. Surely you know that."

"What if she is hurt?" She paused for a deep breath. "Or dead?"

As if on cue, the butler, an aging, dignified man by the name of Quaid, entered and coughed discreetly. "There is an Officer John Smith here to see you, sir."

Hugh and Zoe exchanged a look. It was almost as if by saying the morbid possibility out loud, she had manifested some terrible truth.

Hugh nodded to Quaid. "Show him in."

Chapter Three

It wasn't that she was surprised at what John was telling her. A body had been found. But she found herself strangely removed from the conversation, like when she was a child and would try to listen to Simone and Hugh's conversation through a glass placed on the wall. The sounds were there, and she could hear words, but she struggled to grasp their meaning.

He spoke again, more slowly. "It's your maid, to be sure, Mr. Dovefield. I recognized the bitty scar on her neck. It's Lucy."

John Smith was a Bow Street Officer, more commonly referred to as a Runner, though most of the officers disliked the term.

With his light brown skin and dark wiry hair, he was clearly of mixed race. Zoe had known him several years now, having first met when he was a young constable and she was a child being sneaked into court by an overeager stepfather. He was one of Hugh's favorite officer's, and it wasn't uncommon to see him come around in a professional capacity. He was a cheerful sort, with an easy smile, and a clever twinkle in his eye. Today though, that twinkle was missing. Today they held only sympathy.

As Zoe let his words sink in, her worst fears all confirmed, the floor seemed to sway slightly beneath her feet. She gripped the back of a chair to steady herself, determined not to faint in front of these men.

She had seen death, bodies still warm she had run past in France, her own small shoes stained red with blood. But as horrible as that was, they were strangers. This woman was not; she could picture her face clear as crystal in her mind. This woman was part of the fabric of her life, and her loss hung heavy on her soul.

"How did she die?" The words sounded wooden even to her own ears.

"She was found this morning in

Whitechapel. Dunno how she found her way over there, but she did. Apparently she was found in the gutter, likely run over by a hackney in the fading light. It happens more often than you might think."

Hugh clasped his shoulder warmly, the way men did when they wanted to show affection to a friend. "Thank you for your trouble John. I'll see to it you are rewarded for it."

John inclined his head, acknowledging the compliment. "Of course. The coroner will have to look over the body to determine a definitive cause of death, but right now it looks like an accident, so the body is likely to be released as soon as this evening."

"Excellent. Now we can put this unfortunate business behind us. I would appreciate it if you could arrange for the body to be brought here as soon as it's possible." Hugh turned to Zoe. "You were right, Zoe, and I'm sorry I dismissed your concerns. I know it's not much consolation right now, but at least Lucy will get a decent burial. I'll see to it."

Zoe nodded numbly and turned to go. Something John had said was at the edge of her memory, fuzzy already, but troubling, like an itch one couldn't scratch. Then at the door, she stopped, her mind finally catching up with her intuition.

"Where did you say she was found, John?"

"Whitechapel."

Now that made little sense; she felt her senses sharpen. "Lucy would barely walk with me to Hyde Park. She was afraid all the time of even the safest parts of London. She never would have gone to the worst parts."

John opened his mouth to reply, but Hugh raised a hand to stop him. He stepped closer to his stepdaughter and spoke in a low voice. "Zoe, I know you are upset, but this is over now. It's a tragedy, but there's no need to make it worse than it already is by seeking out trouble when there's none to be found."

Zoe's eyes flashed. "Over? Nothing about this makes sense. What was Lucy doing in Whitechapel, of all places? And 'run over by a hackney'—how can they possibly know that? It sounds to me as though a conclusion has already been drawn and now the investigation, if you can call it that, is just a matter of routine."

"Zoe, you need to calm down. When you

have lived as long as I have and seen the things I have seen, one thing you learn is that there is validity to Occam's razor. The simplest answer is usually the right one."

"But—"

"That's enough, Zoe. There will be no more discussion on the matter. The coroner will make these determinations, not you or me."

His voice had taken on the hard edge that told her this conversation wasn't going anywhere. Frustration boiled inside her, but she contained it. She would get nothing if she lost her temper and threw a fit.

Hugh softened as he looked at her.

"This has been a difficult day, Zoe, and this is difficult news. Perhaps you should spend the next day or two at Theo's."

Chapter Four

Theodosia, as Hugh's older sister, was as much a mother as a sister to Hugh, and had been a vital part of his life after their mother had died in childbirth while bearing his younger brother. Hugh's father had remarried quickly, and baby brother Sebastian was allowed to stay as part of the new fold. His older brother, Baldwin, was married respectfully and patiently waiting to take his place as the next Baron of Newark, and one couldn't rightly ask the heir to leave the ancestral home. Theo was the only child already gone. Beautiful and lively, she had married a much older man, with an enviable title and an even more enviable fortune. So young Hugh, at the age of fourteen, was sent to live with his older sister. It was she who finished raising him into the man he became, paying for his education and supporting him in his decision to become a barrister.

She was still beautiful, witty, and warm. When Hugh brought home his controversial French wife and her angry daughter, Theo accepted them without hesitation. Zoe loved her completely.

Within an hour she was in the carriage Hugh kept for the family, with the parlor maid along for the ride as propriety demanded. Since she would be with her aunt, the maid had been instructed to return home after Zoe arrived.

Hugh must have sent word ahead, because Theo opened the door herself instead of her butler and as soon as she saw Zoe she reached out to encompass her. Theo still stood straight, though time had turned her hair silver. She had green eyes like Hugh but hers were large and round, and with her button nose and ready smile, Zoe could easily imagine her as the diamond of the first water.

Zoe felt tears well up and, to her surprise and embarrassment, she started to cry. Theo held her and patted her back as her sobs continued. When finally they subsided, Theo gently pushed her back and looked into Zoe's red-rimmed eyes.

"Looks like tea isn't going to quite fit the bill, my love. Let's retire to the sitting room where I keep the good stuff."

Zoe smiled through her tears. Theo had taught her many things. Appreciating a fine single malt was among them. Where Theo had learned them, one could only guess, but it was a known fact that her aunt was an eccentric. Her husband, the Duke of Wentworth, died after only six years of marriage, leaving Theo a young, rich widow. She rarely spoke of the time before she was a widow, but Zoe knew it hadn't been a love match. Once she was free of the restriction of a husband, but still retaining a decent part of his fortune, and the status that comes with being a Dowager Dutchess, there was little that could stop Lady Theodosia Bexley, formerly Dovefield.

Once the footman poured the drinks and left, Zoe poured out her heart, for the first time admitting out loud the pressure she had put on Lucy before she disappeared—died.

"There is no excuse for how I behaved. I know that." Zoe kept her eyes downcast.

Theo was silent a moment, then leaned over and, with a finger to her chin, raised Zoe's eyes level. "Then learn the lesson. Embrace the opportunity provided by your own missteps, and learn the lesson. Add it to the lessons learned from other poor decisions, and move on, hopefully better. Staying put doesn't help anyone."

Her aunt leaned back and settled in with another sip. "You know I've loved you since I first laid eyes on you, Zoe. I love the strength your past has given you, and I know the future holds much good. But truthfully, you have been a bit full of yourself lately. I've seen you rude to your cook, dismissive of the footman, and disrespectful to your mother. Lessons are hard, love, but they need to be learned. Having blue blood, whether French or English, is no excuse for bad behavior."

Zoe sighed, but met her eyes squarely. "It's not just Lucy, although this is a terrible thing. Sometimes I am just so tired of being different. This is not my home, even now, after all these years. It's simply where I live." She took a sip of her drink and continued. "It's been hard to always be different. And French on top of it all. There is no love lost here for the French. It's been hard. Perhaps I've become hard in return."

Realizing she was babbling, Zoe rose, taking her glass in her hands and swirling the amber liquid as she collected her thoughts before she spoke. "I know I am fortunate. Hugh has been a true father to me. I want for nothing. But I am still unsettled and angry and demanding. It is not as though I do not see."

"You are fortunate, my love, but don't think for a moment you don't deserve it. You deserve all of it and more. I think you would've benefited from a sibling closer in age, to make sure you knew your place." Theo smiled with warmth. "That's what I had. Someone who would ignore the money and the title and tell me what I needed to hear. Baldwin is a bit of a snob now, but I never doubted I had someone in my corner who would keep me honest. Sometimes I hated it, but it always helped me." Theo paused to take a sip herself.

"I think we've beaten that topic to death."

Theo switched back to the reason for Zoe's visit. "So Lucy came here that day. I never saw her, but Bensen told me you were not coming, and I noticed the flier was gone. I assumed it was retrieved by one of yours."

"She made it here then. But she never came home. I just know this wasn't an accident. Someone hurt Lucy. I just know it." Zoe spoke with passion, and her eyes hardened.

Theo narrowed her eyes and stared at Zoe for a long moment before finally speaking. "If you feel something strongly enough, you have to do something about it. There is little more important in life than being true to yourself. I know my little brother means well when he tells you to leave it alone, but if you truly believe Lucy met with foul play, then you would be doing her and yourself a disservice by ignoring your intuition."

"I just don't know what I can do."

"You are a young woman with all the advantages that come with status and wealth. On top of that, you are intelligent and competent, and most importantly you possess a strength of will to rival any man's. The only limitations that can hold you back are the ones you impose upon yourself."

Zoe stared at Theo, letting her words sink in. She knew she was right; she couldn't let this go. She needed answers. Perhaps John would know where she could get them.

"Is there a boot boy who could run a message for me? I believe I need to speak to a Runner."

Chapter Five

Officer John Smith wouldn't have admitted to being nervous as he waited for Zoe. He might concede to "unsettled" though. The conversation at the Dowager's house had led to the arrangement to meet here. Zoe needed someone who could be hired for a price, cared about truth, and most importantly, was not him. Being in the good graces of someone like Lord Hugh Dovefield was a situation too precious to his career to throw away on a whim.

The cheerful but off key whistling of an unrecognizable tune grated on his ears. John glanced at his cousin. Her mother, Cherry, had asked him to keep an eye on Mary for the day. Being a dutiful nephew, he hadn't the heart or the spine to say no.

At eighteen Mary was in no need of a sitter, but boredom didn't suit her temperament. Truth be told, Mary was fine company, his favorite of his many cousins, with a ready laugh and a quick, unfiltered wit. Her dark, tight curls were pulled up in a neat bun on top of her head, giving her a semi-respectable look. But John wasn't fooled.

"Mind your manners, Mary. Zoe Demas is a nobleman's daughter, and you done brought us enough trouble from noblemen to last a lifetime."

"Why John, there's no need to scold me. You know I always know my place." Despite her flippant words, Mary's smile faltered for a moment.

A pang of regret struck him; John hadn't meant to speak so harshly. "I'm not saying I blame you for what happened, Mary. Blue blood doesn't give a man the right to treat you like that. But you and I, we can't afford more enemies. The world's hard enough for the likes of us."

Mary inclined her head to show her understanding. Like John, she leaned toward a cheerful countenance, usually happy with what came her way. With a bit more Devil may care mixed in, he thought.

John smiled wryly and turned his attention to the Lady Demas, making her way through the throng of Londoners. This part of the city south of the Thames was generally referred to as "over the water," and it wasn't the kind of place respectable, high society women frequented. That said, it wasn't the East End either. Their destination resided on Vauxhall Street, a bustling intermingling of private homes, shops, and manufactories. John himself rented a room at a boarding house not too far north. But it was brave of Zoe to come alone. Bravery, he mused, or foolishness. The girl seemed to brim with both.

Zoe was dressed in a simple, long-sleeved day dress with the popular empire style, her dark hair pulled back and mostly hidden under a large bonnet. The dark blue fabric made her already blue eyes appear fathomless. They darted back and forth, betraying her own nervousness.

"Still no maid, I see, milady?" John's concern for propriety betrayed his genuine fondness for Zoe.

"Not yet, John." Zoe words were clipped. "I know it is quite the scandal."

They had been on friendly terms for some years, and as the young woman already found social appropriateness tedious, she'd taken to calling him by his Christian name early on. John didn't mind, but he'd never found it in himself to return the familiarity, at least not out loud.

He ignored her sarcasm, instead turning to the girl at his side. "Let me introduce my cousin, Miss Mary Fletcher. She's spending the day with me."

Zoe glanced at her, and he wondered what her impression was as she took in Mary's brown skin, several shades darker than his own, as well as her generous curves and twinkling black eyes. He was surprised when she smiled and held out a hand.

"How do you do?" It was meant as a polite greeting, not an actual question. The handshake complete, she returned her attention to John. "Shall we?"

John nodded silently and knocked softly before opening the door. They were expected, so he didn't feel the need to wait for a reply.

The interior was comfortable, furnished

in a decidedly masculine style. A large desk took up much of the front foyer, with a chair behind and two in front. Looking to the left of the desk, the room opened up to a large sitting room with a fireplace, a hob for cooking, and two overstuffed chairs and a single sofa pushed casually in front of it. It wasn't visible, but John knew a single cot was tucked along the wall as well. The walls were a good quality paneling, warm hues of brown and gold, and maps and paintings shared space with framed photographs on the walls. It was a space both professional and personal.

A smallish orange cat was curled in an armchair. It briefly opened its green eyes as they entered, then yawned and lazily went back to sleep. John found the beast unsettling, and at best was neutral toward the creature, though he had known it many years. If a person wanted a pet, a dog was the superior choice, in his humble opinion.

The man behind the desk was also well known to John. The oversize desk and chair fit him perfectly, because although half his body was hidden, there was no disguising he was a giant of a man. Well, perhaps not quite a giant, but he was an unusually tall, broad specimen of the human race. He looked up and smiled as they walked in.

"John! It's great to see you. And little Mary, not so little anymore. It's been a while." His smile remained fixed as his gaze moved to Zoe, but his eyes were less friendly and more appraising.

John spoke quickly. "Good to see ya as well, Quinton. This here is Lady Zoe Demas. Lady Demas, Mr. Huxley. She's in need of services beyond my purview."

"Demas? As in Hugh Dovefield's stepdaughter?"

Zoe answered. "Indeed."

Quinton raised an eyebrow and leaned back in his chair. The motion must've been interpreted as dismissive or rude by Zoe, because her reaction was to raise her chin and meet his eyes, a defiant glint in her own.

"I'll warn you now, Miss Demas, my services don't come cheap. Whatever trouble you've gotten yourself into, it'll take more than a dress allowance for me to fix it."

John winced. The purposeful use of Miss instead of Lady didn't escape Zoe's notice either.

"Money won't be an issue, Mr. Huxely, if

you are a man up to the job." The insinuation was thinly veiled, but instead of further anger, Quinton's only response was a slight quirk of his lips.

The time to make a timely exit had presented itself. "Mary and I will be takin' our leave, but if you want a bit of free advice, here it is." He turned to Quinton. "Miss Demas isn't here for fun, Quinton, and she isn't here for your lip. She has a real problem and money to hire a man to solve it. I don't know any of us down here as can turn down a paying job."

He then turned to Zoe. "As for you, I know it's not my place, Lady Demas, but I've known you some years, so I'm going to give it to you straight. If you got down off that high horse for a minute you might just find yourself standing on some common ground."

John tipped his hat to both ladies. "Now beggin' your pardon, but i have a paying job myself I'd like to keep."

He was at the door, Mary in tow, before Zoe spoke.

"You're leaving?" The surprise was evident in her voice. "I thought you would remain during the meeting."

John understood instantly what she was saying. In his haste to leave, he'd forgotten all about propriety. A lady of Zoe's station could hardly remain in the office of a man without accompaniment. Of course if she'd arrived accompanied, this wouldn't be an issue at all. Poor planning on her part, and John really did have an actual job he needed to get back to.

Irritated, he stewed, trying to come up with a solution that didn't involve him mediating for the rest of the day. But it was his cousin who solved the dilemma.

"I'll stay with her."

John sighed with relief. "Is that alright with you, Lady Demas?"

Zoe gave a slight nod, and John was free to make his escape. Nevertheless, curiosity played on his thoughts, and as he hurried down the crowded street, he wondered how the three of them were getting on.

∽

It was the lady who broke the silence first. "I'm in need of an investigator. My maid has been murdered."

"That's a bold statement." Quinton met

her eyes squarely. "I assume if the coroner has determined foul play to be the cause of death, an investigation is being conducted by the Bow Street Magistrates Court?"

Color darkened her cheeks. He took it for embarrassment at first, but quickly realized his mistake.

"If the authorities believed it was murder and were conducting an investigation, I would hardly need your help, would I?"

This Lady Demas had quite an attitude. It both irritated and amused him.

"Very well. Tell me about her, your maid."

"The last time I saw her was Thursday last—"

Quinton interrupted her. "We'll get to all of that in a moment. No, I mean tell me about her. Did she have family? How long had she worked for you? What was she like? How did you feel about her?"

He had surprised her. "Why does that matter, sir? Surely my feelings for my maid have no bearing whatsoever on who killed her, or how indeed you will find out who killed her."

"On the contrary, milady, feelings are the lifeblood of every investigation, most of all murder. I need to get a sense of who she was as a person, and more importantly what she was to you. I need to know why you're here today before I can determine if I can help you or not."

She hesitated for a moment. "If you insist. Lucy was my maid for almost a year. She had no family that we knew of and no friends either. She simply did her job and left on her half day. She was often afraid, seldom smiled, always berated me for my lack of fear, and never told me a single thing about herself. She is a blank slate, sir, and I cannot fathom a single reason anyone would want her dead. But dead she is."

"And why do you care?"

"What?"

"Why do you care?" Quinton repeated. "She was just a servant, as replaceable as a piece of furniture, except less expensive. You yourself said she was a blank slate, so you didn't even like her. So what if she's dead? Why do you care and more importantly, why should I care?"

Lady Demas opened her mouth, but no sound came out. She snapped it shut, opened it again, and then closed it again. She stood, the color on her cheeks that he now knew was a sign of anger even darker. Finally, she recovered her voice.

"You are an uncouth and foul man, Mr. Huxley. I see no need to continue this conversation."

Quinton realized he may have pushed a bit too far. "Miss, I mean, Lady Demas—"

"He's just baiting you, milady," Mary interjected. "He's tryin' to get you riled up to see how serious you are about this. I've known Quinton a long time, and he's not half so bad as he would like you to believe right now. Sit back down, please, milady."

She started mutely at Mary, obviously weighing the pros and cons in her head. After a few seconds consideration, she sat back down.

"I apologize for upsetting you, Lady Demas." Quinton leaned forward on his desk, his hands clasped together. "I can see that you do care. But I still need to know why before we proceed."

A silence followed his statement. He exchanged a look with Mary. He'd known her since she was a child, and he hadn't realized how grown up she'd become.

"I'll rustle us up some tea while you think on it." Mary rose, reaching out to stroke the cat, who had by now moved to sit on the desk, as she went by. "Hello there, Oscar." Mary did not hold with her family's strongly held beliefs when it came to cats. As with most things, Mary followed her own mind.

As Mary boiled water on the cooking hob, Lady Demas finally spoke. "Lucy was planning on going out that day, but I insisted she go somewhere for me first." Tears welled in her eyes, but she blinked them back with a stiff upper lip that would've made any Englishman proud. "She didn't want to go, but I insisted—I more than insisted. I bullied her into running my errand. And she never came back. I don't know what else happened to her that day, but I do know that my last words to her were unkind. If I hadn't been so bullheaded, then maybe..."

Quinton interrupted. "Maybe, could have, should have, what if. It doesn't matter. You can't take back whatever it is that was said between the two of you, but I can assure you, you aren't responsible for her death. Only one person has blood on their hands, if indeed it was murder."

The lady met his eyes, but differently than before. Instead of defiance and determination, Quinton saw...something softer. Then Mary returned with the tea, placing a scalding hot cup in front of each of them, breaking the moment of connection.

He cleared his throat and returned to the business at hand. Lady Demas told them both what she knew of Lucy, her life, and her death. Quinton listened carefully, asked questions and made careful notes in a small leather-bound notebook.

"Do you know what arrangements your father has made regarding her body?"

Zoe nodded. "Yes. The body was delivered to our home last night. She'll probably be buried within the next couple days, as soon as my stepfather can arrange a plot in the cemetery."

"Then we'll have to act quickly. Since we're now conducting an independent investigation, I would like an independent expert to examine her injuries to determine cause of death. I have someone who's nearly a surgeon I use for these kind of things."

"Very well. My father will be at court all day tomorrow and my mother has several calls to make in the afternoon. Can you bring your expert at 3:00 pm?"

Quinton nodded. "Yes, that should work. Now, before we discuss my fee, I want to be sure you understand what it is I do. I'm not an officer of the court or a constable, nor am I a thief-taker. What I do falls more in the gray end of the spectrum. I'll do whatever is necessary to fix my clients problems, in this case, to clear up the mystery surrounding your maid's death. But I offer no guarantees, nor do I operate with the blessing of the law. Do you understand?"

She nodded. Money exchanged hands and Quinton made a note of that as well. Finally he closed his notebook, wrapped it with the adjoining leather ties, and leaned back to take a deep breath.

Lady Demas spoke into the silence. "You speak like a gentleman, Mr. Huxley. Like you were born to it. Did you grow up near here?"

Mary stilled and glanced at Quinton, who busied himself straightening his desk. "My mother spoke posh, Miss Demas. She taught me."

He offered no other explanation, and the

lady didn't ask any other questions. But he guessed she was wondering at the close friendship between himself and someone like John, and by extension Mary. For someone like her, it was likely a very strange set of companions—not because of the difference in race, but because of the difference in countenance. John and Mary knew their place in the world, and had grown up comfortable in their own skin. That wasn't to say they thought they were worth less than other people. But they weren't ashamed of where they'd come from. They simply were who they were and made no excuses.

Quinton, on the other hand...he had grown up under similar circumstances, but without the security that came with consistency. He was taught how to speak and carry himself as if he came from a higher class of society. But he didn't. He spent most of his childhood on the streets, hustling and struggling like all the other urchins. Yet he was never one of them. He belonged to some space in between, forever operating in the gray.

Lady Demas stood, apparently sensing that the time to leave had come. Turning to

Mary, she gave her a quizzical look, and after a moment, Mary rose as well.

"Thank you for your time, Mr. Huxley. I'll see you tomorrow then."

He also stood, reaching out a hand that she took in a firm grip. "Until then."

"Until then."

Chapter Six

Both Zoe and Miss Fletcher took a deep breath as they exited onto the street. In this part of the city, the air was fouler than near the parks she was accustomed to, but the cooling autumn air did help the scent. Zoe set off with a purpose, waving her hand to signal a hackney. After a brief pause, Miss Fletcher followed along. As they were waiting for one to pull over, Zoe spoke.

"As your cousin pointed out, Miss Fletcher, I am in need of a maid. Do you currently have employment?"

She shook her head. "I worked in a posh house for a few years, but that job didn't suit me. I left on poor terms. No references."

The words were spoken matter of fact, but Zoe could tell there was a heaviness behind them. There was more to that story, but she didn't pry. References weren't particularly helpful to Zoe anyway—she judged on character, not past performance and the opinions of strangers. Her mother might feel otherwise, however.

"Perhaps this job would suit you. I'll warn you though, I am prone to temper at times, my mother and I quarrel, I routinely refuse to listen to council, and my curly hair cannot be tamed. Interested?"

Miss Fletcher laughed, her eyes twinkling. "Well, milady, if we're exchanging honesty, I should warn you as well. In spite of my mother's best effort, I continue to speak my mind and I rarely lower my eyes as befits my station. However, I've been fixing my little sisters hair since I was old enough to braid—and there's six of them. Curly hair I can do. And, not to be rude, your hair barely qualifies."

Zoe glanced at Miss Fletcher's tight curls, a twinkle in her own eye. "By those standards, I suppose you're right."

By this time the hackney had pulled over. Zoe said, "Ride with me, at least as far as my house. If you decide not to take the job, I'll pay for the hackney to take you home."

They both clambered inside and began the bumpy ride across the river. They would have some time to talk.

The young woman cleared her throat, for the first time looking mildly uncomfortable. "All joking aside, milady, you ought to know, I have mouths to feed in my brothers and sisters. My parents 're missing my wages even now. But when I say I left my last post on poor terms, I mean very poor. I don't want to shock your high born sensibilities, so I won't go into detail. All I'll say is the lord's youngest son had very bad manners and when I was dismissed, he was left with a broken nose and blood running down his shirt. I regret losing the wages, but I don't regret what I did."

Zoe gasped. "You broke his nose?"

"In three places I later heard, though that may just have been his bellyaching. He always was such a baby." She shrugged. "There was an uncommon amount of blood though. Had a right time scrubbing it off my apron."

A strangled laugh escaped her lips, despite Zoe's efforts to take the situation seriously. Miss Fletcher smiled, clearly relieved that the story hadn't altered Zoe's opinion of her.

It took her a few seconds to compose herself, but eventually Zoe cleared her throat. "Well I appreciate your honesty. I can assure you, all the men in our home have good manners. My mother would tolerate nothing less."

She thought back to Theo's words. *"You would benefit from someone to tell you what you need to hear. To keep you honest."* From the start she'd felt a kinship with this woman, and though she had no logical explanation for it, she wanted her to stay.

"So are you interested in the job?" she asked.

"I am, if your mother will have me."

"She'll have little choice if she wants me to go everywhere accompanied. My mother and I don't see eye to eye on many things, but I can help her see reason on this. I think she'll likely just be relieved I've agreed to take on a maid at all."

"Then I would be happy to accept, milady."

Zoe smiled broadly. "Oh, Miss Fletcher, we're going to have such fun together."

Miss Fletcher returned the smile. "Please, call me Mary."

Chapter Seven

It had been quite a fight to convince the young Lady Demas of the need to remove the poor woman's clothes in order to do the examination. Quinton understood her horror at such an act of impropriety, for a woman to be seen naked by strangers, and worse yet men. But there was no other way.

Eventually he had convinced her to come out and wait in the parlor with him while his expert—if one could call him an expert—conducted the exam. They had sat the two of them in a strained silence, the girl's jaw set in a stiff line and her eyes blinking back tears. He pretended not to notice.

"Where's Mary?"

Lady Demas looked up, as if from a daze. "She's at her parents' house, packing her things."

"Of course."

They lapsed back into awkward silence. The moments seemed to stretch on into hours, although Quinton doubted that. Eventually, the silence became too much for him.

"Will your stepfather raise the roof if he finds out about this?"

Lady Demas looked at him for a moment and seemed to clear her head.

"You clearly do not know my stepfather. In these years since his marriage to my mother, I have never seen him lose his temper." She paused, then even allowed a small smile. "Regretfully, he has seen me lose mine more times than I can count."

Quinton was genuinely curious. "You are close with him?"

Lady Demas leaned back and regarded him. "Are you close with your father, Mr. Huxley?"

Quinton was taken aback, but in truth he had started this. "My father died when I was quite young."

Lady Demas nodded. "My sympathies.

Mine is gone as well. Murdered in fact as we fled France. But I am lucky. Lord Dovefield filled the role well."

She could have left it at that, but she continued, as if compelled to explain. "After the exodus, I had nightmares. Terrifying images of blood and death. And eyes, staring eyes." Miss Demas paused, her own eyes distant. Then she shook her head as if to chase away images. "When it was just the two of us, I would call for my mother and she would comfort me, holding my hand as she helped me back to sleep. Eventually, the nightmares faded. But it wasn't long after they were married, the dreams started again. At first *mama* came as before, but she became too ill when she was *enceinte*. One night when I woke up screaming, I felt a hand holding my own, and I thought it was her. But it was actually Hugh who sat by my bed, murmuring words to make me feel safe again." Lady Demas shrugged, as if what she had just said was a perfectly ordinary thing to share with a stranger. "After that I always called for Hugh. And he always came."

"He sounds like a good man."

She looked at Quinton, her blue eyes

clouded with memories. "Hugh is the only man who has ever made me feel safe. Even *papa*, who I loved with all my might, did not keep me safe. I still love *papa*, but Hugh is my father now. He is the man I trust."

Quinton was quiet. He was not accustomed to conversing with a stranger about such intimate details of their life. Before he could decide how to reply, the sound of footsteps signaled an end to any further personal revelations.

"You can come in now."

The two of them followed the sound of the Scottish brogue back into the room. Lady Demas's jaw was still set in that hard line, but there were no longer tears in her eyes.

"You don't have to come in," Quinton said gently.

"Yes, I do. I'm better now. I won't be a hindrance again, I promise."

The first thing to hit him was the smell—not of the two-day-old corpse, but of the myriad of flowers that had been arranged around the room to hide the decay. The floral scent was overwhelming; Quinton raised a hand to his nose instinctively and breathed through his mouth.

The poor woman was still unclothed. Quinton reflected that there were few things less human than a corpse. You'd think it would just look like a sleeping person, but there was something distinctly separate about the cold, pale flesh and the unseeing eyes. It should just be a person, but the difference between a person with a soul and one without made all the difference.

Quinton imagined who the girl on the bed might've been, but it was hard. The body really was just a blank slate. Lady Demas had mentioned she'd been quiet and reserved, but there was nothing left of her to confirm or refute that. Just the stillness of death.

"It's always sad to see one so young, aye?" said the other man in the room—his expert—Rory Stewart. His accent was still evident, but nearly two decades in England had soften its edges, making him easily understandable, but with a distinct Scottish charm.

He appeared somewhere in his early forties, with reddish hair darkened by the years. His hair was just beginning to show streaks of gray, but his eyes were still a vibrant green. A leather apron covering an excellent cut of trousers, and a well-tailored shirt and waistcoat. Business was thriving.

"I was thinking the same," said Quinton with a sigh.

"I have discovered a few things." Rory grabbed his hand and guided it down to her forearm. "Can you feel it?"

Quinton resisted the urge to flinch away from the clammy, cold skin and instead pressed down harder, feeling the bone underneath. This close to the corpse, the rotting scent was clearer, and it made him more appreciative of the flowers. The arm was firm under his touch, but as he moved along, he felt an odd bump. He glanced up at Rory for an explanation.

"Broken bone. It's an old injury, probably from childhood."

"Hmm." Quinton swallowed hard and quickly withdrew his hand. "What about the cause of death?"

Rory turned the woman's head and parted her mousy brown hair to reveal a ragged wound. "Blow to the head."

"Hmm. Could it have been an accident?"

"Only if she accidentally hit her head three times." He paused. "Another thing, this girl was no virgin maid." Rory cleared his throat and nodded to Lady Demas. "Begging your pardon, miss."

Quinton blinked. "Really? That is surprising. Are you sure?"

"Well she's definitely given birth, so unless she was the next virgin Mary, I'm pretty sure."

Lady Demas finally spoke. "That isn't possible. Lucy…Lucy never spoke of a child."

"Well I can't tell you what she spoke about, but I can tell you she's definitely given birth."

Lady Demas's eyes narrowed. "What did you say your qualifications are again?"

Rory chuckled. "I didn't."

She turned back to Quinton, her hands on her hips and a glint in her eyes. "I thought you said he was a surgeon."

"No, I said he was *nearly* a surgeon." Quinton clapped a hand on Rory's shoulder. "Mr. Rory Stewart here is in fact a world class resurrectionist."

Her eyes widened. "You mean you've brought a grave robber into my house?"

"A resurrectionist," Rory corrected.

Lady Demas glared at him.

"A resurrectionist," she growled. She took a deep breath to regain her composure, as if trying to resist the urge to stomp her feet. "But what exactly makes him qualified?"

Rory spoke for himself. "As to my qualifications, I don't have any formal education or apprenticeships, but I have learned from the best—even the great Robert Knox."

"What does that mean?" Lady Demas snapped out each word, losing her grip on her patience.

"Well all medical schools need bodies for dissection, and there's just not enough dead criminals to go around. I've been supplying 'em since I was fifteen years old. I'd give them a discount on the corpses if they let me stay and listen and watch. My chance to apprentice with a proper surgeon didn't really work out, and I don't have the bloodline or connections to go to medical school. So I use what I know in a more...unconventional setting."

Quinton interjected. "It might seem a bit odd, but for a situation like this, there's no one better than Rory. Honestly, there's a thing or two most physicians could learn from him."

"I find that quite difficult to believe," Lady Demas voice had gone up a full octave.

"Why would the coroner not uncover these same findings? Surely he has more qualifications than you just mentioned."

"You would be surprised, milady, at the lack of qualifications held by a coroner. The present one couldn't find his own arse in a dark room if he was allowed both hands to do so."

Quinton felt that wasn't fair; the coroner did have some skill. But Rory had more medical background, that was certain. And certainly it wasn't worth a debate. Rory always won debates.

"I will say, Lady Demas, that a body found in Whitechapel of a maid would not get the attention Rory has given her."

Lady Demas said nothing for a moment, then changed the subject. "Can we at least cover Lucy up?"

She waved a hand at the body and Rory followed her gaze.

"I'll cover her, if that's what you want, milady. But that over there, it's not Lucy anymore. Whatever you want to believe about what happens when the breath is gone, that has happened. And I do more than rob graves, as you so eloquently called it. I help people find truth. Sometimes Quinton. Sometimes the authorities. Sometimes family. The body of those gone are now a book to be read. Like it or not, I can read them, and read them well." He turned to the body and covered it gently with a sheet. "*It's not enough to speak, but to speak true.*"

Lady Demas's jaw dropped. "Shakespeare? You know Shakespeare?"

"Aye, well, not everything he wrote is worth quoting, but A Midsummer Night's Dream, that's art." He turned back to Lady Demas and laughed. "I'm not sure if you're more confounded by the fact your maid had a child or the fact a resurrectionist enjoys Shakespeare. Perhaps you might find yourself drawing the conclusion that everyone is a bit deeper than you first thought. Maybe even yourself."

Lady Demas said nothing. She was indeed at sixes and sevens. She stared for several seconds, then shook herself and spoke softly. "I think I need some air."

As she reached the door, she stopped and looked back at Rory. "Thank you for your work here. For the...reading you do."

As she slipped out the door, Quinton let

out a sigh of relief. Rory's Scottish roots left little consideration for the feeling of the aristocracy, French or English. It could've gone worse.

Rory came around from the other side of the room. "There's one other thing. I found a note in one of the inner pockets of her petticoat."

Quinton took the note from him and turned it over in his hand. There was a reddish brown stain he could only assume was blood smeared on it, and the edge was clearly torn. It read: *4:00 pm West*. The rest of the word was torn.

"I think she might've had that in her pocket as she was dying. I don't know if it means anything. That's your job."

"Aye. Thanks, Rory."

He stepped out of the room and saw the girl was waiting on the other side of the door.

Quinton stood near her and cleared his throat. "I'll contact you when I have something to report."

She looked up at him with a gaze that could only be described as forlorn. "I didn't know her at all. She had a whole life and I didn't know anything about it. And Rory. He's right. I didn't even give him a chance. What does that say about me?"

He reached out a hand, almost placing it on her forearm, but withdrew before his senses completely left him. She was a gentlewoman and better than he ever would be.

"It says a great deal that you're here now, searching for answers to questions others would rather not ask."

Lady Demas paused, and when she spoke her voice was low but firm. "I do want answers, Quinton. Whatever those answers are, I have come to need them."

Surprised at the use of his given name. Quinton paused, then inclined his head; he understood, more than most. "I'll keep in touch with my findings."

Chapter Eight

Quinton moved purposefully through the dingy, winding streets. Though the sun was still high in the sky, in neighborhoods such as this it appeared its light couldn't quite penetrate the clouds to warm the ground beneath. The shadows stretched out in sinister shapes, hiding any matter of sins in their icy darkness. A shudder ran up Quinton's spine, and he shrugged his long, woolen coat tighter around his shoulders.

He wasn't usually so easily unsettled by the old neighborhood; after all, he was not a stranger to these streets. He had grown up in those same shadows. But this job had unnerved him more than he cared to admit.

It was not unusual that his business should lead to dealings with the upper class—indeed, their world collided with the slums more often than some might believe. But most of Quinton's acquaintances of that class were gentleman; second or third sons caught up in some mild scandal or refusing to pay debts, etc. For a lady to have ventured so far beyond the boundaries of society was most unusual. For her to risk her reputation—something more valuable than money amongst those of that breed—over a mere servant was unheard of. It spoke to a strength of character that Quinton couldn't help but find intriguing.

His destination suddenly appeared before him, and he dismissed such thoughts of the dark-haired Lady Demas from his mind like smoke on the breeze. Even when his attention was elsewhere, Quinton's feet knew where to go.

The sound of his knuckles rapping against the worn wooden door was nearly lost in the echoes of the East End—carriages creaking, horse hooves clopping on the cobblestone, babies crying, men arguing, women bartering. It was a familiar din and most of the time Quinton naturally tuned it out, but today it seemed especially loud.

The door opened slightly, allowing a single eyeball to evaluate him through the crack. It didn't take long for them to recognize him; Quinton was a distinctive figure at over six foot tall, with shoulders as broad as most doorways and hands like dinner plates. The door swung open, revealing a skinny youth covered in pox scars and missing several teeth.

The boy gestured for him to enter, and Quinton followed him up the stairs. He was not a stranger to this address, but it was not entirely familiar to him. It wasn't the home his friend had grown up in, and by extension himself. This was a proper home, not just a crowded tenement teeming with vermin, both human and animal alike. Of course, he had been grateful for any form of shelter over his head. Time had changed things for both of them.

When they reached the top of the landing, the subject of his undertaking came into view and the youth discreetly faded out of view.

"'Ello, Quinton old boy. What an unexpected pleasure. Would you care for a drink?"

"Alright then, Charlie." Quinton removed his coat and hung it on the rack, then settled himself into a chair across from his friend.

Charles Modi sprawled out across a couch, holding a glass filled with a generous measure of golden liquid, and a cat-like grin on his face. He rose gracefully, filled another glass with the same generous portion, and handed it to him, before relaxing back down onto the couch.

Quinton took a sip, the cool whiskey burning his throat and then warming his stomach. "You better hope your mother doesn't catch you with this."

"I'm a grown man. I don't need my mother's approval." Despite those brave words, Charlie shifted uncomfortably. "Besides, she is out on a house call with *Bahan*. They won't be back until this evening."

"Lucky you."

The two men had grown up like brothers, though they could not have looked less alike. Where Quinton was big as a carthorse, with light skin, brown hair, and light brown eyes, Charlie was slight, much like his mother, barely coming up to Quinton's chin, with the same dark eyes, thick black hair, and bronze skin.

Looking at them as youths, people had always assumed Quinton was the protector—that is, until they saw Charlie's temper in action. Auntie had done her best, but that vicious streak never left him. Eventually, as the boys grew older and made their way in the world, their paths had drifted apart. While Quinton walked the line between both light and dark, Charlie had established himself quite comfortably in the darkness. He was king in his own right of his little corner of London's underworld, a place he had fought relentlessly to carve out for himself.

"So, what brings you by, Quinton? You never visit the old neighborhood unless you need something."

It was a fair criticism, so Quinton got straight to the point. "A girl was killed three nights ago. The body was found in Whitechapel." He took another sip before continuing. "She was found a street over from your newest gambling den."

Charlie's eyes narrowed; one inky black and the other pale white. A scar ran from his hairline to his jawline, a constant reminder of the incident that left him blind in his left eye. It was a memory that still woke Quinton up in a cold sweat some nights. Many flinched away from his unnatural gaze, but Quinton held it evenly.

"Why are you asking me about something like that? Do you really think I would have anything to do with that?"

"Charlie—"

"We've known each other fifteen years and you think you can talk to me like this?" Charlie stood, his voice rising in volume. "Just accuse me of killing some girl like I'm a stranger in a pub?!"

"Charlie, calm down—"

"Get out of my home!"

By this time Quinton had also risen and was backing away. Charlie's eyes were far away, and he knew that when Charlie had that look about him, he couldn't trust his old friend to reign in his temper.

Just then he heard a door slam shut, followed by the stomping of small feet up the stairs. Charlie's eyes refocused, as if his soul had returned, and his features took on a guilty expression. Quinton recognized it from their childhood and there was only one person who could inspire it.

At only one and a half meters tall, some might underestimate the woman standing before them. That was before they saw the lightning in her eyes and the storm clouds in her expression, or felt her tongue slice them open like a razor. Few people intimidated Charlie Modi, but his mother made the short list.

In his defense, Katyayini Modi was a force to be reckoned with. Not only had she raised her own two children alone in a foreign country, but she had opened her door to her son's feral friends. Quinton knew he likely would've turned out very different if not for the tiny Indian woman.

"You dare to speak to your *Bhaee* like that?" Her eyes widened. "And are you drinking, as this time of the day? You are always belligerent when you drink. Sit down, Quinton, sit, sit."

Quinton cautiously reseated himself. "Of course, Auntie."

She was not done with her tirade. "Here your *Bahan* and I have been out, delivering new life into the world, and you're here drinking away our earnings!"

"My earnings," Charlie muttered under his breath.

Her eyes narrowed into black slits. "What did you say, *Beta*?"

Charlie was no fool—he knew when he'd been bested. He sighed and flopped back onto the couch. "Fine, you win."

"Obviously." Auntie Katyayini turned her attention back to Quinton. "Now what do you need, *Beta*? Have you eaten today?"

"Yes, Auntie, I already ate." Of course, this was a lie, but he knew it didn't really matter. She wouldn't believe a word out of his mouth, anyway; the tiny woman had already bustled off to the kitchen.

There was still another woman remaining in the room—Charlie's sister, Savita. She grinned and flopped down onto the couch beside her brother in a very passable imitation of his dramatics.

"So what are you doing here, Quinton?"

"I came to ask for some advice from your brother, but I stuck my foot in my mouth, as usual."

"You mean my brother's temper got ahead of his brain...again." Savita smacked Charlie lightly on the shoulder. "There's no reason for you to be difficult, not with Quinton. Don't be rude."

Charlie sighed again. "Well since I'm clearly outnumbered...you wanted to know about a dead girl?"

"Yes. A lady's maid by the name of Lucy Wright."

"North or south of my new business venture?"

"South."

Charlie frowned. "That's unsettling. But you know how it is there. Anyone could've killed her—just because I have a few boys in the area doesn't mean they had anything to do with it."

Savita broke in. "None of Charlie's boys would do something like that. They know he'd kill them if they did."

"I know, Savita." Quinton turned back to Charlie. "I just wanted to ask if you could put out some feelers—see if anyone saw anything. I don't even know if she was killed in Whitechapel. Could be the killer just dumped the body there and hoped no one would look too close, considering the reputation."

"Alright, I'll ask the boys. It isn't perfect,

but I try to keep some sort of order. If someone in my sphere interfered with that girl in anyway, I'll take care of it."

Quinton sighed and shifted in his seat. "Just ask around and let me know what you find out. DON'T take care of it. I'd prefer to take care of it my way, please."

Charlie waved a dismissive hand, but before Quinton could reiterate his point, Auntie Katyayini burst back into the room, carrying a tray nearly her own size filled with Indian pastries, curries, and sweet smelling chai tea.

"Eat, eat, eat," she said, gesturing to the overwhelming amount of food.

Quinton knew better than to protest further; besides, there was no telling when he would get to eat her food again. He reached for a samosa, only to have it snatched out of his fingers by delicate brown fingers.

Savita sat back, a self-satisfied grin on her face. "So, how is John these days?"

"Don't start!" Charlie groaned.

"He's good, Savita." Quinton struggled and failed to hid his amusement. "I'll tell him you asked after him."

"Please do."

Chapter Nine

Zoe smiled as her younger sister ran ahead to enter Hyde Park. Walter was already ahead, and she called out for him to stay close. She was much older than either her half brother or half sister, but she was still fond of them. Growing up in France, she longed for a sister and remembered begging her mother for one more than once. Simone would smile and say that Zoe was all she and her father ever needed, but Zoe never tired of asking. Later, in the tiny flat on the east side she and Simone had called home for years, she longed even more for someone to share the long days when her mother searched for work. In time, she resigned herself to finding her way alone.

When her mother and Hugh wed, and Walter was born the next year, she was secretly thrilled. Three years later when Phoebe was born, she remembered holding the tiny baby in her arms and feeling the connection that could only come with family.

Of course, reality soon set in that it would be some time before the wailing infant in her mother's arms would be a confidant or friend. Even now, though she enjoyed the children, it was usually at arm's length and for short periods of time. They were simply too young to be considered peers. But today the crisp fall weather beckoned her, and she had invited the children to come along for a walk. Mary walked alongside her, easily carrying Zoe's artist's easel, not falling into step behind as was the custom for a maid, but instead walking in stride with her, brightly commenting on the foliage of the park.

Many people entered the park through its northwest entrance, which was judged to be the most beautiful part of the park. It was flanked by Kensington Gardens and the Serpentine River, and had a fence to exclude carriages. But Zoe preferred the southern end of the park, close to the Serpentine, where in the summer all classes of people came to bathe, and in the winter an equal amount came to skate. Fortunately for Zoe's preferences, the cool fall weather had cut the masses. As they strolled, Mary asked a question.

"How old is that butler of yours? He seems absolutely ancient."

Zoe laughed. Quaid was indeed a fixture at their stately home. He certainly predated her.

"He is south of seventy, but by how much I cannot say." She paused and looked at Mary suspiciously. "Why do you ask?"

Mary tried and failed to look innocent. "I may have sent him a few years closer to his Maker last night, though I assure you, no harm was intended."

"What on earth happened?"

She continued. "I have a routine I do at night, for my skin. Most times I apply a bit of Bloom of Olympia before bed. It helps keep my skin soft and keeps away wrinkles and I love the smell. Like heaven itself."

Zoe looked at her, slightly confounded.

"Your skin is exceptional, Mary, without blemish. I have often found myself envious of the beauty of your skin."

Mary stopped and placed the easel on the ground, leaning it slightly on her leg. "Exactly." She pointed in a circular motion at her face and hair. "This does not just happen. It takes effort, and routine. Once a week, before bed, I apply a paste, made from ingredients on the islands, used by the women of our family for generations."

This statement was accompanied by a shrug of the shoulders that made Zoe wonder which London drugstore sold the island elixir.

"I apply it thickly, and the white color stands out a bit on me. But last night, after I applied it, I got to thinking of those ginger biscuits your cook does make. They will melt in your mouth, those biscuits. And I found myself peckish. So I slipped down the servants stairs to see if I could acquire a biscuit or two. When I rounded the corner in front of the kitchen, I came face to face with your south of seventy Quaid. I was traveling a bit faster than perhaps I should, as I full fronted the man before I could stop." Mary paused for effect. "I just do not believe he is used to seeing a woman of my complexion in motion with a white paste covering her face. And it was also unfortunate that I had loosed my hair as it continued after I stopped, effectively blinding him."

Zoe pictured the overly proper but decidedly elderly Quaid bouncing off Mary's curves, fighting Mary's rather voluminous hair while wondering what horrid mask she was wearing, and laughed. "What did he do?"

Mary sighed. "It was the scream that made me realize my error. Like a frightened girl, he shrieked. I think he thought I was a ghost. And the flailing. With my hair in his face. he may have thought that to be the substance of the ghost in his face. But the damage was done, so after he composed himself and made his way out of there, I was able to retrieve the biscuits. Cook was still laughing when I left, tears streaming down her face. I'm not sure my relationship with Quaid will ever recover."

Zoe laughed harder, leaning on a tree for support until finally she could stop. She shook her head at Mary and started walking again, an occasional laugh still escaping.

They found a pleasant space not too far from the walking path, and Mary set up the easel. "How would you like it placed? I know the light makes a difference to you artists."

"Light is everything, Mary. It is all important. Fortunately today is a gloriously sunny day, so if you will place the easel facing the water, perhaps my sister will stand still long enough to sketch her, and I can capture the light on the water as well."

While Mary set up the easel, Zoe arranged her pencils. She had three handmade graphite pencils, each custom ordered for her sketching. When she first began drawing, she used a quill and inkwell, and sometimes at home she still enjoyed the calming routine of sharpening the quill to a fine point before beginning a sketch. But the portability of the pencil was priceless. She arranged the pencils and drew out her paper.

Of course she had her paints and brushes with her too, but today she felt the urge to sketch. Lately, faces were fascinating to her. The planes of the cheekbones and the depth of eyes caught her attention. She thought of Phoebe, and the way her eyes mimicked their mother's eyes, the resemblance more pronounced with each year. She herself favored her father with her tall slender frame, but she too shared her mother's eyes. Perhaps she could get the girl to sit for a quick portrait sketch.

The thick sheet of paper was on the easel when she heard a horse approaching. Zoe glanced up to see a man was astride a beautiful bay. He brought the beast alongside her and Mary with the skill of a true horseman. His features wore a pronounced smile.

"Good day to both of you lovely lasses." The Irish accent was pronounced, but the words were understandable. "A day for artists I take it."

Mary moved closer to Zoe, keeping her eyes on the interloper. He was a middle-aged, clearly Irish gentleman. He was wearing a fashionable top hat with the latest semi bell crown, but Zoe could see his hair was still red where it wasn't streaked with gray, though Zoe suspected in his youth, it might've been even more fiery. His riding breeches were of a fashionable cut and his riding boots polished to a shine. If the magnificent horse did not make it obvious, this was a man of money.

Zoe said nothing for a moment, surprised to be approached so boldly by an unknown man. Certainly it was customary to gain an introduction before speaking to a lady. But, she reflected, perhaps the rules were different in Ireland. The Lord knew she herself, as a foreigner, had breached English etiquette more times than she could count.

"It is a fine day, sir."

Walter, drawn to the beautiful horse like a moth to a flame, ran up to them.

"Can I pet your horse?" he asked, his green eyes aglow.

"Aye, he's a gentleman. He'll not bite ya."

As Walter moved toward the horse, Mary quickly placed herself between him and the Irish gentleman.

"Stay close to me," she whispered.

True to the gentleman's words, the horse was gentle as they stroked his nose.

Zoe eyed Mary in surprise as Mary continued to maneuver herself between the man and Walter. She did not meet Zoe's eyes, but murmured quietly to either Walter or the horse. Zoe glanced back to the man.

He appeared not to notice, his smile still in place and his blue eyes twinkling at Zoe. "Your boy is a natural with the beast."

"My brother, not my boy," she said

quickly. How old did the man think she was? She tried not to take too much offense. Her mother often told her men were very poor at guessing such things.

"Of course, I apologize."

By now Phoebe had joined Mary and Walter at the horse's side, but Mary was no longer focused on the horse. She finally met Zoe's gaze, her eyes agitated. She raised her eyebrows and jerked her head subtly towards the road. Clearly any Irish charm was lost on Mary. She wanted to leave.

Zoe's brows furrowed. She didn't understand what Mary's problem was.

She looked at the gentleman again. He was staring off at something in the distance, allowing her to notice the planes of his face. His cheekbones were high, making his face angular. Not exactly handsome, she thought. But interesting to be sure. His light eyebrows sloped downward, wrinkles marring the corners, making his eyes look even more deep set, accentuating the vivid blue. Her fingers twitched, aching to draw him.

His attention refocused back on her. "I'm not from around here, as I am guessing you

THE TIES THAT DIVIDE

surmised. Lord Patrick Driscoll, at your service. And you milady?"

Zoe answered without hesitation, the famous British manners she had fought against thrusting themselves to the fore. "Lady Zoe Demas."

"Pleased to make your acquaintance, Lady Demas." Lord Driscoll walked back to his horse and gathered his reins. "I won't be bothering you any more than I already have, milady. Just wanted to say hello. My rented house is along the same road as yours, I believe. I have seen you out walking before. My son and I ride out regularly. He has gone ahead, so I had best catch up to him. Time for me to give my horse his head."

With that Driscoll vaulted onto the saddle, surprisingly agile for a man of his age.

"Good day." He tipped his hat, turned the horse, and trotted away.

"What on earth is wrong with you?" Mary snapped at Zoe. She could practically feel the agitation rolling off her.

"Wrong with me? I was about to ask the same of you. He was hardly the devil incarnate, just overly friendly! Why did you take such an immediate dislike to him?"

Mary faltered, but only momentarily. "I had a feeling is all. But you should know better than to chat away with any 'overly friendly' man who smiles your way."

Zoe frowned, ignoring the scolding. "A feeling? What kind of feeling?"

Mary hesitated again, then spoke quickly, the agitation causing her accent to become more pronounced. "I can trace my family back a long ways, back to da islands, and even all da way back to Africa. Not on paper, but passed down, mother to daughter, over and over again. All through my family line, there's stories of some who had the sight."

"I myself don't have the true sight, but I believe in it. Every now and then I get a feeling so strong I canna ignore it. It's not exactly a voice, but I can feel it telling me something. That Irish man, I did not like him. I can't explain it, but I know evil travels with him."

Zoe had hung on every word. "Well I won't dismiss a women's intuition, sight or no sight. My own has saved my neck a time or two. Fortunately, we likely won't be spending too much time with Lord Driscoll."

Mary inclined her head and then changed

the subject. "Do you still want to sketch the lass?"

Zoe smiled at Phoebe, but shook her head. As Phoebe chased after her brother, Zoe focused her attention on sketching the middle-aged, red headed Irishman whom Mary did not like.

Chapter Ten

John leaned back and sighed deeply. There was a weariness about Quinton's old friend that diluted his usual cheerfulness.

"Tough week?" he asked.

In the blink of an eye, John's face transformed into his usual smile, the weariness erased. "Not particularly." He changed the subject. "You know, it always feels like home in here, Q. Like I can take off the clothes I wear in public and be myself here."

Quinton smiled; John was the only person he knew who called him Q. "I will say I'd much prefer you keep your clothes on, but this place is home to me, too."

He let the topic go, but he noted his friend didn't feel enough at home here to take off all his clothes—the mask of optimism remained firmly in place. John had been that way since he'd known him; always the cheerful one, the peacemaker, the optimist. Heaven forbid his own troubles should darken his friends doorstep.

A gust of night air suddenly chilled the room. "Thought I smelled a good whiskey."

As Charlie closed the door behind him, Quinton slid another glass from a drawer. He offered it to him, and the three moved to the fireplace without speaking a word. Being in front of a warm fire was always a place of comfort for them; they remembered all too well the times they'd had none, huddled together for warmth when times were leanest.

Not every Friday evening found them here, but once or twice a month, the boys who had grown into men followed their feet back to each other. It hadn't really been planned that they would come here; Quinton's work/living area simply offered the best space for them to relax—John's boarding house was too crowded, and Charlie's home had a mother peeking over their shoulder.

The unspoken rule was they left their jobs at the door. Any revelations shared over whiskey inside these four walls was sacred. They were children of the street again, bound and bonded by everything that came with such a heritage.

Even Charlie, with his quick temper and shifting mood, calmed here. He sat in the overstuffed chair closest to the door and smiled as Oscar the cat unfolded herself from the arm of Quinton's chair and meandered toward him.

"Traitor," muttered Quinton, though the corner of his lip quirked upward.

"They never forget who saves them," replied Charlie, stroking her fur as she settled on his lap. "I wasn't sure she would even make it when I dropped her off. Starved little thing. I wanted to take her home, but we all know mother doesn't care for her kind."

"Katy always had good sense," John said under his breath.

Quinton laughed. "I've never understood your unease around Oscar. She's hardly a harbinger of doom."

They'd had this discussion before, so John

said nothing, just shook his head and took another sip of whiskey.

"John and my mother hold to older superstitions than you or me, as irrational as they may be." Charlie paused as Oscar's purr became a quiet roar and her blazing green eyes squinted with pleasure. "The real mystery is how she is a girl. In all my time since, I ain't never seen another orange cat twas a female."

Charlie prided himself on his precise enunciation and grammar. It was the kind of thing one learned with a British father who taught you for the first six years of your life. But every once in a while, the cockney accent he'd grown accustomed to the other thirteen years slipped its way in. He didn't wear the expensive, tailored clothes that Rory Stewart did, but his clothes were nicer than most in Whitechapel—well kept and clean in the baggy pants and shirt and vest that befit his Indian heritage. His lifestyle was hardly respectable, but he was desperate for respect. He wanted so badly to be taken seriously.

"We all believed that until the kittens came. All four orange as could be, and all four male. She's an exception to be sure." Quinton smiled at her fondly. "Even with her poor judge of character, she's been fine company."

Conversation turned to family, naturally leading to the subject of Mary. John told Quinton and Charlie how well she fit in with working for Zoe.

"It's been awhile since I've seen her quite so cheerful, and with some money to help to boot. Lord Dovefield's wages are more than fair."

"I'm sure he has to pay extra for that stepdaughter of his. Help is probably hard to keep. She has spoiled written all over her." Quinton offered a refill for his friend's glasses with a nod of the bottle. His words were harsher than his actual feelings. In truth, the lady had grown on him over the short time they'd spent together. She was headstrong, but hardly a monster. He thought of what Zoe had said about being close to her stepfather, and felt a small pang of guilt, but still felt reluctant to speak kindly of her to his friends. He knew they would grasp at any reason to tease him.

John was thoughtful in his reply as he swirled the golden liquid in his glass. "Lady Demas is a bit spoiled, I'll give you that. But she means well. And Lord Dovefield has always cared for her like his own." He paused to sample his filled glass. "You wouldn't know it to look at her, but she's been through a lot. And she is French. That makes her..."

"Moody."

"Passionate," John corrected him.

Charlie snorted. "I don't know why we're wasting conversation and good whiskey debating the moral high ground of some aristocrat."

Quinton and John took the cue and turned the subject away from Lady Demas and over to the more compelling things.

"How goes your inquiry into the maid's death?"

"I haven't had a lot of time to unravel that yet. Rory says it was murder, so that's a start. But I have other clients. Right now there's two other people asking me for some legal advice, and I have been tracking down a few things for them."

John opened his mouth as if to say something, but then glanced at Charlie and shut it. Instead he leaned back into his chair, content for now to listen.

Quinton continued, "Rory also said she carried a baby to term."

Charlie raised an eyebrow. "Well that opens up some possibilities. Nothing like the responsibilities of fatherhood to inspire violence in a desperate man. I've seen it often enough."

"True. I also know Lucy ran an errand for Lady Demas that day, so I need to work from there. Some Aunt's place was involved. I plan to go question the staff on the morrow, after I take a look at where the body was found."

"I might be able to help there," said John. "I was over near the Dowager's yesterday on other business and one of the girls was quick to talk about the murdered maid. Honestly, for the likes of me, I do not see what is with women and gossip."

Charlie interrupted. "If you listen to the women in my house, they will inform you that men are the gossips. That the sole purpose of men's clubs is to have a place for men to hear the latest *on dit* with the appropriate refreshments." He held up his glass as he spoke, enjoying the same refreshments here. "They might have a point. Isn't it kinda what we do?"

Quinton laughed. "That is a valid argument, but let's not share it with any of the women we know."

John rolled his eyes. "Anyway, the maid told me that Lucy did stop at the house and talked to the butler. Then Lucy started on her way but she got into some kind of spat with a footman. I figured I'd pass that along to you anyway, but now knowing Lucy had a bairn, that does put it in a different light."

"Very helpful, John. Thank you." He rubbed his chin, reflecting on his friend. "Being a runner becomes you. You're good at it."

Charlie snorted, but John ignored him and smiled. "I bet none of us thought back when we were young'uns that I would end up with a respectable job. I'm not sure how any of us managed to get where we are."

"Most of those we ran with are dead." Quinton looked at Charlie. "Really, it was your mama that made the difference. Without her, I'd be lain alongside the rest. I owe her my life."

"It's true, she saved us all, I'll give you that. But only I have to put up with her harping. Her and Savita both." But both other men saw the softness in Charlie's eyes that belied the words. No one could doubt how he felt about his women. "Nowadays you both just eat her curry."

John laughed, and he and Quinton shared a look. "That curry. I dream of it sometimes. I remember being alone in that tiny flat at night with my mama gone workin', and the smell of your mama's curry would come down the stairs. Most days there weren't food in my belly and I would follow that smell right up to your place. Your mama would set me a bowl with you and Savita. To this day I've never again had a meal so filling."

Charlie was apparently also in a mood to reminisce. "Her work as a midwife fed us in those early years, and she still makes her way, Savita learning now." He looked at John. "After a while mama just yelled for you down the stairs at night. Hardly remember eating without you there for a few years. Til your mama died and you moved to your cousin's place. When you weren't sleeping in a doorway somewhere."

John's voice was relaxed, the years softening the desperation he felt.

"Cherry tried, she did. But she had enough mouths to feed and was always expecting another, and Uncle Morgan wasn't much of a worker. You know what it's like on the streets. Eight or nine years old, you better be ready to be a man. But I found my way to your mama's table regular enough to keep me alive. She never turned me away, and the floor by the fireplace was always there if the nights were cold."

Quinton spoke next. "I well remember that floor. I was on my own when you both ran into me and must've taken pity on me. I didn't have much of anybody back then. The first time you brought me home, Charlie, your mama took one look at me and started putting food in front of me. When my mama was alive we always had full bellies. She was a talented actress. Even after my father died, we never really lacked for anything. But I was eleven when she died, and like you said John, eleven on the streets is a man."

The whiskey was passed along again, and the mood became even more reflective. It wasn't the first time these stories were told, but the telling of them always seem to tighten the threads of their shared lives.

"We didn't take pity on ya, mate." Charlie chuckled softly. "You already was bigger than either of us, with feet like a grown man. We figured if we could keep you alive, you would be on our side in a fight."

"You proved us right many times" John laughed as well. "It's a wonder we all kept from getting dead and even built ourselves a life. You've done well for yourself, Q. This place fits you like a good pair of boots."

"Lord Coleville was generous after I did that job for him early in my so called career. I was working on word of mouth only, with no place to work out of except my boarding room, and he told me this building was mine for a reduced rate, since it was just sitting empty anyway. It suited my needs fine. When I get enough squirreled away, I may approach him to see if he would sell it to me."

"He must have taken a shine to you, for sure. A lucky break, but we've all seen a few of those. Apart from mama, it's why we made it from beggars on the street to respectable men." Charlie smiled broadly, his white teeth gleaming. "You two slightly more respectable than I perhaps."

All three laughed, the whiskey making them mellow. Oscar unfurled her small body from Charlie's lap, stretched, and leaped to a sill and then out a small window that was left open a few inches. Charlie took that as his cue, and departed, promising to bring a bottle next time.

John paused before following him out. "One last thing, Q. I didn't say anything because I know how sensitive Charlie is about the higher ups, but you might consider asking Lady Demas about those legal questions. She spent half her childhood at Old Bailey watching her step-daddy at work."

"Really? Dovefield took her to Old Bailey? As a child?"

"Mm, Mr. Dovefield took her regular alright, a bit behind her mama's back. She was caught up with birthing the new bairns, and Mr. Dovefield spent time with Zoe. That's where we met. She were right intense about learning and Mr. Dovefield was just as willing to teach. I didn't make a fuss about her being there, and Mr. Dovefield has given me work ever since. Girl ought to know the law up and down at this point."

Quinton was astounded, though he tried not to let it show on his face. That girl was like an onion, layer after layer to remove to find out who was there. Or a gift, he thought. A wrapped gift. He shook off his thoughts and got back to the case.

"She is full of surprises."

"That she is." John pulled his coat on and tipped his hat. "Goodnight, Q."

Quinton returned to his place by the fire and poured himself a last glass, staring at the amber liquid as it swirled in his glass. But he dismissed thoughts of Lady Demas from his musings, at least for the evening. He had other things on his mind.

His life really had been quite a ride 'til now. Talk of his mother always raised her from the far-away corner of his heart where he kept her tucked away. He let himself feel her arms around the boy he had been, holding him close and telling him tales of the man who died—his father. He thought about how much she loved them both, even though his father was years dead. The love showed in her eyes when she spoke of him. Quinton remembered the way her eyes twinkled when she told him as a small boy that his father was special, different, and that made Quinton special, and one day she would explain all. And then she was gone—not only gone, but viciously and suddenly ripped from the world.

Quinton knew what she meant. Even though he was only three when his father died, there were a few vague memories of a blurred face and the scent of sandalwood. He had one clear memory of his father, his back to them, and his mother gazing at him, the love clear in her eyes. He knew his mother meant that one day he, too, would find a girl whose eyes would light up when she looked at him. A woman who thought he was special too.

Not yet though. There had been a few ladies, to be sure. One of them held his heart longer than most, but that, too, ended in heartbreak. And no one had ever looked at him the way his mother looked at his father.

He wasn't special yet.

Quinton sighed and downed his drink, folding his memories back into their tiny corner where he could bear the loss. Even after all these years, it was still raw and painful. It was that pain that had driven him to his current path, helping those the law could not. He'd always hoped that one day her murder would be solved—he'd even tried for a while, begging the ancient case notes off John. But nothing had come of it. It had been too long. Whoever had taken her life still walked the earth, breathing air that should've been hers. The thought filled him with rage, as hot and destructive as the fire in front of him.

A mew from Oscar brought Quinton back to his senses. She was sitting in the window, contemplating him with an unreadable expression, her tail twitching back and forth. She was right, as usual. It was time for bed.

Chapter Eleven

The smell of human and animal waste was brutally strong in this part of Whitechapel. Quinton's lip curled in disdain as he watched rats scurrying along the walkway, crawling over a lump that could've been mistaken for a discarded heap of clothes, but which he knew to be a discarded person.

Quinton didn't know how Charlie could stand to stay in the old neighborhood. There were many disease and vermin riddled sections in this city, but nowhere made his skin crawl like here. It was where the lowest of the low ended up—where those with no other options wasted away in the dark shadows, away from the judgmental eyes of a society that preferred to pretend they didn't exist.

He finally dismissed his dreary thoughts as the place where the maid's body was found came into view—it wasn't relevant to his task at hand, and the faster he did his job here, the faster he could leave.

John said she was laying in the gutter of Plum Tree Street. The name was misleading—no plum trees, or vegetation of any kind, grew along its sides. It was a depressing place to end one's life; disposed of like a piece of trash in the filth of the street. A chill came over him, and it wasn't from the damp autumn weather.

Quinton wasn't sure what he hoped to find here, several days after the incident, but he always went to the scene when a job involved a true crime. Sometimes it felt as though the place itself was changed by it, as if the violent act had changed the energy of the air itself. Sometimes he could almost see it happen, picturing the series of events in his mind..

But there wasn't much hope here. Too much time had passed. The body was gone, and the scene cleared of anything resembling evidence. But he didn't have the luxury of an abundance of leads, so here he was on a cramped, plumless street in front of a crumbling tenement, hoping against hope that inspiration would strike.

He couldn't see them in the darkened windows, but he knew there were dozens of eyes watching him. The sheer density of population in areas like this guaranteed there was always someone watching. If Lucy had been killed there, someone would've seen it.

From what Lady Demas had described about the maid, it didn't seem likely to him she would've come to this part of London of her own volition. Even if she did have some secret business that would bring her to Whitechapel, Plum Tree Street had nothing of interest. There were no shops or markets, just tenements.

The more he thought about it, the more likely it seemed that she'd been killed elsewhere and then dumped on a quiet street in the notorious area. Even so, it would've been difficult to carry a body, even with two people, through here without someone noticing.

As a former resident of the neighborhood, he knew even if anyone had seen something, they probably wouldn't be particularly disturbed by it. They certainly wouldn't be seeking out a constable to share their account. But if what Quinton suspected was true, and she'd been killed elsewhere, then it was also likely the real murderer wasn't a resident of the neighborhood. Not understanding the culture of the area, they would've feared watching eyes and loose tongues.

So a body dump, done quickly and efficiently. One couldn't just hire a hackney for this sort of thing. They would have to have access to private transportation; perhaps the killer had money or status, or at the very least was adjacent to someone who wouldn't notice a carriage being taken out in the dead of night. Quinton thought of the Aunt's footman who argued with Lucy—it was a possible a servant could pull it off, given the right set of circumstances.

An image of a hackney rattling along the cobblestones came into his mind. It would've been dark; there weren't any streetlights, so the only illumination would be from the lantern on the carriage itself. They slowed down just enough to shove out an awkward shape, speeding up again as the form slammed into the pavement with a wet thud. He could almost see the poor girl laying there, her unseeing eyes staring up at him with an accusatory look. But then he blinked, and the image was gone, and all that was left was the muck and mire of a cramped, dark street, seen in the cold, gray light of early morning.

A flicker of movement out of the corner of his eye made Quinton glance over his shoulder. For just a moment he could've sworn he saw a figure slip into a doorway—for a moment he was sure he saw a boy, thin as a rail and pale as a ghost, huddled there, clutching a rag around his shoulders in a hopeless effort to stave off the early morning chill. But then the moment faded and his past reflection faded with it, leaving a young girl in his place.

She was small, looking to be around the age of ten, give or take a few years to account for malnutrition. Her skin and matted hair were so buried under layers of dirt that it was impossible to tell her ethnicity, or to discern any distinguishing facial features. She was a formless and faceless creature of the streets, but that suited urchins. There was safety in being invisible.

None of his observations were remarkable, except for one thing. Even from a distance, Quinton could see a glint of gold around her neck. That didn't belong in this setting—he was amazed no one had killed the girl for it.

Dark eyes glared out at him, sizing him up as he approached. She didn't flinch—she didn't move at all. Somehow despite the clear difference in size and power, Quinton got the distinct impression in the equation of predator and prey that in this case he was not the predator.

"What does the likes of ya want?" she said. At least, that's what Quinton assumed she said through her thick cockney accent.

Quinton crouched down in front of her, careful to stay out of striking range. The fingers on her left hand were gripped tight around something hidden in the folds of her threadbare shift. If he were a betting man, he would bet on a knife, or more likely, a sharpened piece of metal that she would use as a knife. The child was a survivor, and survival came at a harsh price.

He reached into his pocket and drew out a half-eaten meat pie wrapped in a handkerchief. Asking if she was hungry was demeaning, so he just held it out wordlessly.

Her eyes narrowed in suspicion. "What do you want for it?"

"Nothing. You take it, and I'll tell you what I need. Then you can decide if you'll help me or not. I always find I make better decisions on a full stomach."

Starvation left little room for principles. She snatched it out of his hand and began consuming it like a wild animal.

Between mouthfuls, she said, "Nothin' is free, least not 'round here. Tell me what ya want."

Quinton understood the sentiment all too well, so he got to the point. "Five nights ago, someone dumped a dead girl, right over there. I don't suppose you saw anything?"

She shrugged. "I see lots of dead people."

"I'm sure. But this would've been…more unusual than the dead people you're used to seeing. She wasn't from this neighborhood. A carriage would've brought her here, late at night."

The child shoved the last of the pastry into her mouth. "Was she 'portant? Like a lady or somethin'?"

Quinton thought about it for a moment. "She wasn't a lady, but she was important to someone. I'm supposed to figure out what happened to her."

"Hmm." She licked her fingers, savoring the morsel. "I saw a carriage come down here. I only 'member 'cause I never seen one on dis street before. I thought they must've been lost."

"Do you remember the dead woman?"

"I 'member a couple a dock workers taking a somethin' to the pub the next day, but not a dead woman specific."

"What about the carriage? Was there anything distinctive about it?"

She shook her head. "It was dark."

Quinton repressed a sigh. He'd known going in it was a long shot, so he had little right to be disappointed.

"What about that?" He pointed to the gold chain around her neck.

She clutched at the object. "It's mine."

He held up two placating hands. "I believe it. I'm not going to take it. I just want to know where you got it."

A tense moment passed while she considered this. Quinton held his breath. Finally she gave a slight nod. "A lady came here, thinkin' nothin' of it, maybe a couple days ago. She left flowers. That was wrapped around 'em."

That was a fascinating piece of information. If someone had come here to memorialize the maid, they must know her. Anyone who could offer some information about her past would be invaluable.

Quinton cleared his throat, trying to keep his voice even. "Could I take a look? I promise, I'll give it right back."

She shrunk back, clearly not trusting his assurances. He reached into his pocket, pulling out the golden pocket watch he always carried. "Here, you can hold this until I give it back."

The girl hesitated, but clearly she wanted to hold the hefty chunk of gold. Finally grubby fingers snatched it out of his hand and quickly replaced it with the delicate chain.

Attached to the chain was a round locket. Quinton ran his fingers over the cool metal until he found the catch and opened it up. Inside was a miniature portrait of a beautiful woman. He recognized her immediately, a surprising thread connected to his own life. On the other side was an inscription:

Dearest Abigail, Thank you for everything. With Love, Lucy.

The pieces clicked into place. He didn't know how the maid knew someone like her, but it was a starting point at least. A wave of relief washed over him.

"Thank you for your help." He handed the necklace back to the girl, and she reluctantly exchanged the pocket watch for it.

Feeling the weight of his precious object back in his hand, his stomach churned with a pang of guilt. There were so many lost souls living in the underbelly of the massive city, it was hard to even fathom. It was easy to let the scale of the problem wash over a person, becoming numb to the suffering of thousands, even when you once shared their plight. But it was harder to ignore when you were looking into the eyes of a single, starving child. He could not help everyone—but he could help her.

"What's your name, child?"

"Gwen."

"It's nice to meet you, Gwen. My name is Quinton."

He fumbled in his coat pocket, pawing at the loose coins until he felt the right one. He pulled out a silver crown and held it out to Gwen. Her eyes widened, and she reached out tentatively to take it. For someone like her, a crown was more than she might ever see in a lifetime.

A sudden blow from the side knocked him down. Quinton gagged as his hands slid across the muck, trying desperately to catch his fall and keep his face above it all.

He scrambled to his feet, fists clenched, prepared to fight the thug that was clearly threatening him. But when he turned, all he saw was a boy. He was older than the girl, maybe five years her senior. He was thin and malnourished, but despite that he came up to nearly Quinton's own height, which was no small feat.

It took a moment of deep breathing, but Quinton slowly unclenched his fingers. He would not beat a child, no matter how disgusting his overcoat now was.

The boy turned to the girl and gestured at Quinton, but he made no sound other than a grunt.

"It's alright." Gwen moved to stand between them, but only looked at the boy. "He didn't hurt me. He just wanted to look at m'-necklace."

"I didn't want—"

Gwen interrupted him. "You have ta look at my brother when you're talkin'. Ezra can't understand you otherwise. He's deaf."

"Oh." Quinton cleared his throat and turned his head to look the boy straight in the face. "I meant your sister no harm. I just gave her some food and a coin for letting me look at the necklace."

The glare on Ezra's face could've melted iron. Quinton didn't blame him. Many men wouldn't hesitate to exploit a defenseless child. If this boy was the girl's protector, then he couldn't afford to give a stranger the benefit of the doubt.

Quinton took a step back, but didn't turn his head. "I'm sorry for the misunderstanding."

The glare didn't soften, but the boy's shoulders relaxed slightly. He gestured again at his sister. She watched intently and then turned back to Quinton.

"He wants to know if you're gonna take da necklace."

Quinton looked again at the boy. "No, it's yours to keep. I have what I need."

The boy gestured again, and again Gwen translated for him. "The next time ya need something, he wants ya to go to him, not me." She leaned toward him and held up a hand so Ezra couldn't see her lips. "He's a bit overprotective, but I think you're nice. Ya can ask me for help if ya need it again."

A smiled ghosted his lips. "I'll keep that in mind."

Chapter Twelve

The sound of pounding against solid wood woke Quinton from a dead sleep. At first he actually thought the pounding was coming from inside his head. But as his senses came back to him and his eyes adjusted to the light, the sound continued.

It had been too late the day before to pursue his lead, but the prospect of spending the evening alone was too much to bear. So his feet had led him to Charlie and the two of them had stayed out far too late, drinking far too much cheap ale.

He clambered out of his cot, his head aching and his mouth dry. Oscar stood and stretched from Quinton's bed. She yawned lazily, perturbed more by his movement than by the noise, and wandered into the main room, sitting down and looking back at Quinton.

Throwing on his breeches over his smalls, Quinton realized he was still in his shirt from the night before. Just as well, he thought as he stalked to the door. Throwing it open, two things astonished him. First, that the sun was shining brightly—not to mention painfully—in a midday sky, and second, that Zoe Demas and Mary stood in that midday sun.

"You look like the devils of Hades, Mr. Huxley. Are you in any condition to speak about my case?"

Quinton blinked, unable to form an appropriate response. He felt the words pound on his brain like the fists that had pounded on the door, his ale addled brain too sluggish to process what was happening. Ignoring him, Lady Demas and Mary entered.

"Actually I am in no mood to discuss a thing, as I am feeling poorly," he said in what was intended to be a firm tone, but in reality came out as more of a hoarse whisper. "I'm not even dressed."

Mary had the gall to laugh. "I have too

many cousins and brothers to be fooled by you, Quinton Huxely. I know a man who spent the night before in his cups better than most, and I got no sympathy for you." She looked him up and down, her lip curled in disapproval. "I'll start the tea."

That was the end of any reasoning with Mary. Quinton cleared his throat and turned to the other intruder, trying to pretend he hadn't lost control of the goings on in his own home. Although his dry mouth wasn't entirely disinclined to the idea of tea.

"Miss Demas, this is how it works," he growled, his voice starting to sound more like himself. "You hire me. I do the work. You pay me. We do not need constant discussions. In fact, you can wait happily at home and I will send word when I have anything relevant to share."

"Have we met before, Mr. Huxley?"

Quinton blinked in confusion—perhaps he was still drunk. "What? Of course we've met before."

"Ah, good. I wasn't sure if you remembered, since you seem to have me confused with someone else. I do not wait for things to happen, or for someone to decide what is relevant to share with me. Lucy was my maid and I will be privy to her investigation."

In the time it had taken her to dress him down, Lady Demas made her way over to his fireplace, which Mary was in the middle of lighting. She busied herself dusting off one of his armchairs with a handkerchief before settling herself down into it. The self-satisfied expression on her face put Oscar to shame.

Irritation, exasperated by the difficult woman and his own discomfort, boiled up inside him. "I am truly at my wits end, Lady Demas. I am in no mood to explain how I conduct my business. Please take your leave before I forget my manners entirely."

His words may have had more power if the room wasn't spinning as he spoke them, he thought. To undermine his authority further, he sank into the armchair across from the lady. That Charlie would answer for this.

But as Quinton's head rested against the back of the chair, he knew the blame rested squarely on his shoulders this time. He had sought Charlie out and refused to go home in the wee hours of the morning, when even his friend was done. The thought of going home with only his own thoughts and memories for company had compelled him against all wisdom and reason to push himself as close to oblivion as was possible while one still breathed. What on earth was wrong with him?

He opened his eyes to Lady Demas glaring at him, a thunderstorm behind her dark blue eyes. If it weren't for those brilliant eyes...

"I demand an update, and I won't leave without one."

"Give the man a minute." Mary straightened up and brushed off her dress, having succeeded in her efforts with the fireplace and the kettle. "You'll get nothin' out of him in this state, trust me. Let's have a spot of tea and then we can talk."

Quinton could see from the set of the lady's jaw that she wanted to argue, but to his amazement, she held her tongue. Mary must have some kind of magic to silence that one. Within moments, all three held steaming cups of tea. Quinton didn't know how the Frenchwoman felt about tea, but he knew for an Englishman, there were few things more restorative. He sipped the soothing beverage, feeling his demons drown in the excellent blend.

It didn't take him long to finish the first cup. He handed it silently back to Mary, who refilled it just as silently. Quinton let out a deep breath; he was ready.

"Very well, Lady Demas. What is so troubling to you that you've barged your way into my home?"

Her eyes flashed, but when she spoke, it was without the fire he expected. "I have been plagued by her death, sir. I cannot sleep, I barely eat. This woman who shared the majority of my waking moments for a year—I barely knew her. I am asking you, please, can you give me an update?"

Quinton was surprised. He looked at the lady carefully. Without the haze of leftover drunkenness, he was able to note the dark circles under her eyes. She seemed thinner, too. The familiar pang of guilt twisted in his gut—he hadn't considered the toll this may have been taking on her.

"I do have an update, milady," he said, his tone gentler.

He told them about the urchins and the necklace. Over the course of his tale, Lady

Demas moved closer and closer, until she was seated on the very edge of the armchair.

"So perhaps this necklace will lead us to the killer?" she said, her excitement barely contained.

"This necklace is simply a clue. I will follow it up tomorrow. I am afraid this day has already been spoken for. You were right to be critical—I've wasted half a day on my own demons, and now I have other appointments I cannot reschedule."

His honesty surprised even himself, but it was true. He could admit when he'd made a mistake.

"Very well. Mary and I can accompany you tomorrow." Her eyes danced and met Quinton's own. The clouds in them were gone. Storm abated, he thought. When he was a boy, his mother had taken him on a trip to the sea—this confounding woman's eyes were the same color. He knew no other eyes that could change like the sea, one minute gray and stormy, and the next bright and blue.

"I will come to your house tomorrow early. We will go from there." No one was more surprised than Quinton to hear the words spoken aloud. What on earth was wrong with him? He never took clients along for the ride.

But it was too late to back out now. The lady smiled—a brilliant, wide smile that transformed her face. Quinton swallowed hard. There would be no going back now.

Chapter Thirteen

When Mary woke her to say that Mr. Quinton Huxley was asking for her at the servants' door, Zoe was genuinely shocked. He said he would come to pick them up, but she wasn't sure he actually meant it. She thought it was just one of those things men say to placate a woman when they no longer wished to discuss a topic.

It was an unholy hour, but Zoe leapt out of bed and Mary dressed her in record speed. She didn't want him to get bored and leave because of a delay.

She raced down the stairs as quietly as she could, Mary following a step behind. At this hour, only servants were awake, but she didn't want to risk waking her parents, or her noisy siblings. Not that she was afraid of the confrontation—no one who knew her would accuse her of that—but Zoe would rather have it after the fact than before.

She imagined Huxley was waiting for her in the kitchen, his arms crossed and his foot tapping. But as she rounded the corner, in the moment just before he saw her, his expression was relaxed, his large frame leaning against the wall as if he had not a care in the world. Zoe knew he was objectively a handsome man, but her heart skipped a beat when she saw him this time. The memory of him laughing came to her mind unbidden...

Then he saw her and his demeanor changed. His relaxed stance disappeared, replaced by the stiff shoulders and sour expression she recognized from their first encounter.

"I hope you aren't going to scowl at me the whole time," she quipped cheerfully.

His eyebrow raised. "I am not scowling."

"You're scowling," added Mary.

Huxley's expression remained stern, but Zoe thought she saw a faint quirk in his lips.

"Let's just go, before your stepfather wakes and has me arrested."

The three of them slipped out the door and onto the street. Huxley had a hired hackney waiting, and they quickly climbed in. It wasn't until they rounded the corner of the street that Zoe exhaled a breath she hadn't realized she'd been holding in.

"Okay, where are we going?"

Huxley ran his fingers through his hair. "What's the last play you saw?"

Zoe squinted. "What?"

∼

As they pulled up in front of the new Covent Garden theater, Zoe smoothed her dress. It was last season's style, with a floral pattern on a light blue wool that was meant for the cooling autumn months. It was still flattering, but hardly her most fashionable dress. If she had known she would meet the great Abigail Swanson this morning, she would have taken more care in her choice of clothes.

Huxley disembarked first. There were no footmen with a hired hackney, so it fell to him to be the gentleman. He reached up a hand to assist the women down—there was no way to refuse it without being unforgivably rude.

Zoe swallowed her discomfort; she would not be the one to flinch. She grasped his gloved hand firmly. The size of it dwarfed her own, yet his grip was surprisingly gentle.

As soon as her feet touched the ground, she withdrew her hand. She hadn't been too bothered by the weather before, but suddenly her hand felt...cold. Zoe cleared her throat and made space for Mary, but not before she caught the amused look on Mary's face out of the corner of her eye.

The tension stretched out for a single, unbearable moment, before Mary broke it. "Are we going in or what?"

Huxley cleared his throat. "Of course. The theater is still closed this early in the day, but they'll let us in around the back."

He led the way around the magnificent building. Zoe had been there before, of course, though mostly to the old one. Anyone who was anyone in society went to the theater. This was the newest, grandest incarnation of Covent Garden; the last one burned down the year before. It had only been open a month, but it was already the talk of London society.

In her many times attending the theater, both here and at Drury Lane, she had never entered in the back. Despite the purpose of their visit, Zoe couldn't help but feel excited to get a peek behind the curtain.

Huxley knocked on the door. It swung open almost immediately, revealing a man twice the size of Huxley, which was no small feat considering his bulk. Neither man said anything; the larger one just stood aside, allowing Huxley, and by extension Zoe and Mary, to enter.

"You certainly seem known here," Zoe whispered as they wound their way through the dimly lit corridor. She wasn't so naïve that she didn't know men used the theater for purposes other than on stage entertainment and socializing.

"You could say that," he replied nonchalantly.

She chose not to pursue the subject.

It wasn't long before they stopped in front of a closed room. A soft light shone from under the door.

Huxley rapped his knuckles softly against the door. "Abigail?"

Zoe was surprised. Abigail Swanson seemed like the kind of woman destined to become a rich and powerful man's mistress, maybe even a future king's. Being on close enough terms to use Christian names with someone like Mr. Huxley...seemed beneath an actress of her status. Not that it was any of her business—it really shouldn't bother her at all.

"Come in," said a soft voice from the other side.

The door opened to reveal a lavish dressing room, decorated in plush velvet and soft pink and ivory colors. A woman sat at a makeup table, her back to the door, still facing the mirror. Her face lit up when she saw Huxley in the reflection.

"Quinton!" She leapt up and wrapped her arms around him in a stunning display of impropriety. Zoe had never even seen a married British couple behave that way in public.

To his credit, Huxley didn't seem embarrassed. He turned to Zoe and Mary. "Abigail, this is Lady Zoe Demas and her lady's maid, Mary." He turned back to the actress. "Lady

Demas—Mary—this is Miss Abigail Swanson."

Zoe smiled and inclined her head. "I have to say, Miss Swanson, I am a huge fan of yours. Your performance two months ago as Lady Macbeth, it was...inspiring."

Abigail inclined her head in acknowledgment of the compliment. "Hopefully it's even better this evening, now that Mr. Kemble has finally settled the price dispute."

"Mr. Kemble—he's the manager?"

"Indeed. He raised the prices for tickets, to help make up for the cost of building a new theater. Obviously, it didn't go over very well. But we're all just relieved the issue is finally settled and we can go back to doing our jobs."

"Right, of course."

Abigail smiled and fell back gracefully into her lounge. Zoe had seen her before, from the distance of the audience. Sometimes distance blurred things—made them seem more perfect than they were up close. That wasn't the case with Abigail Swanson. Somehow without the costumes and the makeup, under close scrutiny, she was even more beautiful.

She had those perfect blonde ringlets, the kind that were even and smooth and shiny.

They framed her face in the way ladies spent hours trying to attain. Her big, expressive green eyes filled her heart-shaped face and her full lips were just the right size. She was the kind of woman men fought and killed and died over. If she had been born a hundred years ago in France, she would've been an emperor's mistress.

"So Quinton." Abigail turned her attention back to him. "Are you just here to show me off, or did you have a purpose in coming here? You rarely visit without a purpose."

"That isn't fair." Huxley rubbed his hands together and looked around the room; if Zoe didn't know better, she would think he was anxious. "But in this case, you're correct. The body of a lady's maid was found in Whitechapel. Someone left flowers at the site, tied together with a locket—a locket that held a portrait...of you."

Abigail's ivory skin went a shade paler. "Ah, I see. What's your interest in the maid?"

Zoe thought that was probably her cue. "Lucy was my maid. I've hired Mr. Huxley to investigate her death."

"Oh, I see." Abigail sat silent for a few moments, her eyes glazed over with a faraway look. Zoe opened her mouth to ask another question, but Huxley gestured sharply, clearly indicating he would prefer her not to interfere with the process. Zoe followed his lead—this time.

Finally Abigail spoke. "I did know her once."

"What could that possibly mean?" Mary had been silent from the conversation too long.

"I take it she never spoke of her past, Lady Demas?"

Zoe shifted her weight from foot to foot. "Um, no, we never really...no, it never came up."

She leaned back, settling deeper into the velvet cushions and sighed. "Lucy gave me few details, but someone from her past was a threat. I know she was very afraid, and made a conscious choice to run away to London. She was a brave girl."

"I'm sorry Ms. Swanson, it doesn't sound like the Lucy I knew." Zoe swallowed hard. "She was timid and conservative—she spent half her time scolding me. And I know for a fact she came with stellar references. My mother wouldn't settle for anything less."

Mary raised her eyebrows in amusement, and Zoe amended her statement. "Most of the time."

Abigail hesitated. "I know who your stepfather is, milady. I have no desire to be arrested for fraud."

"I'm sure Ms. Demas understands the need for discretion regarding this conversation." Huxley gave Zoe a meaningful glance.

There was that posh way of speaking again. Zoe knew there was more to his story than he was letting on, but she understood what he was asking.

"I have no intention of repeating this conversation, Miss Swanson."

She looked to Huxley, who nodded his reassurance. "Very well. Lucy and I met about two years ago. I found her one night, half frozen in the alley, and my conscience got the better of me. I gave the girl a helping hand, doing odd jobs around here. And for a while, things were good. She was a timid woman, but I think she was happy. I know we were friends."

"So why'd she leave?" asked Mary.

"To put it bluntly, there wasn't a place for her. She didn't want to be an actress or socialize with the patrons. The odd jobs weren't something that could support her long term, and she couldn't stay at my flat." Abigail gave Huxley a look that he seemed to understand. Zoe wondered if he was her patron, paying for her accommodations. She wouldn't have thought he could afford that.

Abigail continued. "She couldn't stay here, so I helped her leave. I knew a forger who owed me a favor. That's where we got the references. And I knew the Dovefields' were looking for a lady's maid, and that seemed better suited to her temperament. So that was that. She accepted the position and left."

A silence hung over the room as the group processed her story. Zoe felt sorrow well up inside of her. She wasn't angry with Lucy. She was just sad.

A thought occurred to her. "Was the person she was running from the father of her child?"

Abigail's face paled. "So you know about Simon?"

Huxley replied. "We know she had a child. We don't know where the child is." He paused, his gaze scrutinizing. "Do you?"

Abigail was quiet for a long moment. "I do. We kept it hidden as long as possible, but she was pregnant when we met. She would say nothing of the father. I helped her arrange outside care for the bairn. When I heard of Lucy's death, I wrote a letter to inquire after him, but haven't heard back yet. I've been debating what to do—Lucy spent a small fortune paying for his care every month. It's not something I can keep up long term."

Zoe thought of Lucy's frugal ways and felt a sadness fill her. No wonder she'd been so careful with her monies—she was scraping by to pay for her child's care. She remembered commenting on Lucy's worn clothing as she was headed for her half day, and asking why she did not wear the castoffs Zoe gave her. Lucy had made no comment, simply looked at the floor, but now Zoe realized she must have sold them. Zoe felt like a true heel. She had never looked even a single layer deeper, to see Lucy as anything but the person who did what Zoe wanted.

Abigail continued. "I have the address of the home he's at. Simon deserves better." She paused. "Lucy deserved better." She handed a slip of paper to Zoe. "The home of a Mrs.

Lowe. Perhaps you have the means to arrange care?"

Zoe nodded wordlessly, grateful for an opportunity to make up for her callous behavior in the past. Huxley nodded as well.

"Thank you for your help, Miss Swanson."

Chapter Fourteen

"There is no shame in sitting this part out."

Lady Demas scowled. "Don't worry, I won't make a scene and faint or anything of that nature."

Quinton rolled his eyes but held his tongue. He'd told her their destination would be upsetting, even to those with the strongest of constitutions. If the lady wouldn't listen to his advice, then the consequences were on her own head.

"She's fine, Quinton. She doesn't need to be wrapped in silk," said Mary.

"To be frank, Mary, I don't think you should be here either. You may have lived a more worldly life, but I doubt even you have been privy to what goes on behind a baby farms doors. At least I hope you haven't."

The women exchanged a glance, no doubt silently communicating their impatience with his attitude. But they didn't know and there was no way to express with simple words the horrors that might await them.

He didn't really know how bad it would be. The address Abigail had given them was in a decent neighborhood—not where anyone posh lived, but not Whitechapel either. The quality of baby farms ranged from decent places for children to live and be cared for to hellholes where hope and kindness went to die. In his experience, it tended to be the latter more than the former. For many of the women who ran the homes, it was simply easier to pocket the money and neglect the children entrusted to them.

They arrived at the designated address, and Quinton turned to his companions. "If you both insist on going in, just remember to keep any judgments or criticisms to yourself until *after* we have the boy. Let me do the negotiating."

"You act as if we're going to war against an enemy battalion."

Quinton swallowed his first response. "If you wish to wait here, it's not too late."

This time it was Lady Demas who rolled her eyes. She brushed past him and up the steps to the front door. Quinton followed after, taking two steps at a time to catch up, with Mary close behind.

Zoe raised the brass knocker and knocked it against the house three times. Within a minute, the door opened, revealing a wisp of a girl who couldn't be older than twelve. Her dress was plain and worn, and she wore a white cap to keep any loose strands of mousy hair out of her eyes. The broom she held in her hand confirmed her occupation as a housemaid.

"Can I help you?" she asked in a soft voice.

Zoe opened her mouth to reply, but Quinton rushed to beat her to it. "Is the mistress of the house here? We have urgent business with her."

The girl knew better than to speak her employers whereabouts to strangers. "Who may I say is calling?"

"Mr. and Mrs. Cooper."

"Wait here." The door closed and footsteps could be heard hurrying away, presumably to get further instruction from the woman in charge.

Lady Demas stared at him with her mouth open. When his eyes met hers, she snapped it shut. "Why did you lie, and more importantly why did you tell her we were *married?*"

"Keep your voice down," he hissed. "We still don't know why Lucy was killed, but if her child was a part of the motive, I don't want anyone who connects her to this place to trace the boy back to us."

"Fine. But then why did you tell her we were…"

"Because only a respectable, married couple would be looking to adopt a child."

She didn't have time to argue further before the door opened again.

"Please follow me," said the maid.

They did as instructed and followed her into a sitting room. The furniture was in poor taste—gaudy and opulent—but Quinton could tell it was of decent quality and well maintained. The mistress was clearly doing well with her earnings. She sat in an overstuffed chair, her hands clasped across her lap, her hawkish features intently focused on them. She smiled in what he assumed was her approximation of friendly and gestured for them to sit.

"Good afternoon, Mr. and Mrs. Cooper. My name is Mrs. Lowe. Would you care for some tea?" She knew the most likely reason they were there and was likely already counting her money.

"Mrs. Lowe, a good afternoon to you as well. Some tea would be lovely." Quinton removed his hat and placed it on the end table beside him. Despite his size, the sofa felt as though it would swallow him as he sank into it. His pretend wife sat next to him, perched on the edge to avoid such a fate. Mary chose an armchair and seemed to fare better.

Mrs. Lowe ordered the tea and then turned her attention back to them. "Forgive my impertinence, but since we aren't known to each other socially, I assume you have a purpose in calling today?"

"You assume correctly." Quinton cleared his throat, as if gathering his courage to continue. "Mrs. Lowe, your reputation precedes you. I think you likely know why my wife and I are here. We've been married now for five years, but no children. We've discussed it a great deal and having a child would mean the world to us. Since it doesn't seem to be in God's plan for us to have our own, we're seeking out alternatives."

"I see." Mrs. Lowe appraised them, taking in the tailored cut of his clothes and the fashionable style of his wife's dress, not to mention Mary who hadn't been introduced yet. "And what do you do for work, Mr. Cooper?"

"I'm a clerk at a trading company. My wife was a lady's maid before we were married, but now of course I provide for her." A clerk was respectable enough to explain his clothes without warranting further scrutiny, and a former lady's maid would keep cast offs of her mistress, explaining her fashionable dress.

He scrambled to come up with an explanation for Mary. "And this is Miss Anderson. I apologize for not introducing her to begin with. Should we come to an agreement today, she would be our nanny."

Mrs. Lowe acknowledged Mary with a nod and hurried back to the couple. "Hmm.

Well I do understand your desire, but I would like to know how you became aware of my reputation personally? Most of the couples I work with correspond by letter before coming here."

Lady Demas interjected—she was nothing if not quick on the uptake. "I'm afraid I'm to blame for the rush. I've been so distraught and consumed with this, ever since we were wed. Then a few nights ago we went out to dinner with some friends of ours and they recommended you. It seemed like an answer to our prayers. I just couldn't wait to move forward after that, but I apologize if I've done something wrong."

"No, no, not at all Mrs. Cooper. I do not blame you for your distress or your desire to start the next chapter of your life." Mrs. Lowe took a sip of her tea. "May I ask the name of your friends?"

"The Smiths." Quinton swallowed hard. It was such a common name; he could only hope she'd dealt with one at some point.

She immediately relaxed. "Of course, the Smiths. Lovely couple. Well now that we've gotten to know each other a bit, why don't you tell me what you're looking for in a child."

"We want a boy," said 'Mrs. Cooper' quickly. "Under the age of two."

"I see. Well we have a few boys staying here who fit that criteria. You do understand the situation of the children who are available?"

"Yes, the Smiths explained." Quinton smiled broadly. "We know that some of the children here have mothers who are no longer able to care for them and want them to have a better life. We love the idea of providing one of them a loving, stable home."

Mrs. Lowe returned his smile in a way he could only describe as predatory. "Excellent. I'm sure I don't have to explain the nature of these fallen women to you—very unreliable and irresponsible loose women. It's not the children fault, of course, but in fact I'm caring for most of the children here out of the kindness of my heart since their mothers have stopped sending the monthly fee."

Quinton swallowed the bile in his throat. "Of course. We applaud your charitable spirit."

"I don't do it for praise—after all, it's the Christian thing to do." Mrs. Lowe waved the maid over. "Milly, go collect the boys. Get Malcolm, Simon, and Terrance."

His heart skipped a beat at the mention of Simon, but he did his best to keep a neutral expression.

Lady Demas rose. "I'll go with her."

The blood drained from Mrs. Lowe's face. Quinton reached out a hand and gripped her forearm tightly, instinct overriding social correctness. "Dear, I think we should let the girl do her job. Let's just wait here."

He could see that she wanted to argue with him, but something in his eyes must've persuaded her more than his words could. She nodded and let herself settle back onto the sofa. Mrs. Lowe breathed a subtle sigh of relief and gestured for Milly to get on with it.

They chatted for a few minutes, drinking tea and speaking about nothing important. Quinton knew what she was doing—stalling so the children would be presentable when she showed them off.

After an unbearable amount of time, Milly finally reappeared with the three little boys in tow. One was just a babe in her arms, and the other two toddled behind in the way small children did.

Their clothes were semi-clean and he could see the smears on their faces where dirt had been wiped away. Quinton had to admit, they didn't seem too undernourished, and the older two babbled away happily. Lucy likely used to come regularly to see her son, so it was in Mrs. Lowe's best interests to keep him healthy.

Mary took the baby from Milly's arms and bounced him gently. Lady Demas played her part well and sat down on the floor to play with them, oohing and awing over them the way a woman did with children.

A strange feeling came over Quinton as he watched her with the little boys—both happiness and sadness all mixed together. It was like getting a glimpse into her future, when she had her own family and life and was contented with such things. But in his vision, his place on the sofa was filled by someone else.

He shook the melancholy feelings off and focused on the task at hand. Lady Demas seemed particularly fixated on one of the boys —a ruddy-cheeked little thing, with fiery red hair with a faint white streak starting at his forehead.

"What is this one's name?" she asked casually.

"That is Simon. He's such a lovely little boy."

"And what about his mother? Is she in the picture at all?"

"No, I'm afraid she's gone to God. The poor little lad hasn't any family left."

She was at least honest about that. Quinton pulled out his pocketbook, feeling slimy and foul. "How much?"

Mrs. Lowe's eyes lit up; she would not ask any more questions. It didn't take long for them to negotiate a price of ten pounds. Within the hour, they walked out of her home, having purchased a child.

The three of them walked in silence for several long minutes. Even the little boy, held in Mary's arms, seemed to sense the need for quiet contemplation. He looked around with wide green eyes, his big head lolling from side to side, but he didn't make a sound.

"Well, that was something else," said Mary, breaking the silence.

"It's an unfortunate reality of life in the city." Quinton pulled his coat tighter against the cold. "That was one of the nicer ones I've seen. Lucy obviously wanted the best she could for her son."

"I thought she was a perfectly horrid woman." Lady Demas wiped away a dirt smear on little Simon's cheek. "I can't believe it's legal for her to just sell those children. She didn't even have proof his mother was dead."

"It's a murky area as far as the law goes. For now, there's really not any better alternatives for unwed mothers with small children. If they don't have family who are willing to help, and most don't, then they have to do what they have to do."

"I'm not blaming Lucy. I just think Mrs. Lowe was a perfectly horrid woman and I hated her." Lady Demas took a breath and composed herself.

"How did you know which babe was Simon?" Quinton asked, switching the subject.

"He has his mother's bone structure." She shrugged. "I'm good with faces."

"Good to know."

"Regardless, what do we do with little Simon now that we have him? I cannot take him home and I assume you are not equipped to care for a toddler?"

"No. But I know someone who is."

Chapter Fifteen

Zoe accepted the heaping plate of food. "Thank you so much, Mrs. Modi. This is amazing."

The tiny Indian woman laughed and patted her hand. "You are such a lovely girl. Quinton always has the best taste in girls. Charlie, why couldn't you be more like your *Bhaee*? Bring home a nice girl who likes my cooking?"

"Mother, please." The man Huxley had introduced as one of his childhood friends waved his hand dismissively, though Zoe could see color on his cheeks.

When Huxley had suggested bringing little Simon here, Zoe hadn't expected this.

He had encouraged her and Mary to go home and let him handle it, but curiosity and stubbornness compelled her on. Her curiosity wasn't disappointed.

The two men stood side by side, but the differences between them were striking, even ignoring the differences of race. While Quinton Huxley was tall and broad, Charlie Modi was shorter and slight. Huxley's face was often brooding, but nevertheless symmetrical and handsome, with a straight nose, thoughtful brown eyes, and a firm jawline. Not that Mr. Modi had no handsome features, but it was hard to see past the savage scar that started at the top of his hairline and ran through his left eye and down to the middle of his cheek.

The two of them sat in armchairs; every time Mrs. Modi would turn her back, her son would pour something out of a flask in his and Huxley's cups. It was like getting a peek into the past, to see them behaving like naughty schoolboys.

Mary had taken to the floor with his sister, Savita Modi, and both were absorbed in playing with the toddler. Mary and Savita were clearly friends of a sort as well. The atmosphere was relaxed and familiar, as if Zoe had walked in on a private family moment. She didn't know if she should feel awkward for intruding or honored at her inclusion.

When Mrs. Modi was distracted, Mary leaned over. "So what do you really think of the food? I know you English don't have much in the way of a broad palate."

"You keep forgetting, I am French. I think it's incredible." Zoe meant it, but in truth the heat was burning a hole through her mouth. She wondered if the others could see sweat on her forehead.

"It can be overwhelming if you're not used to it." The younger Miss Modi took her plate, scraped what was left onto her own, and handed it back in one graceful move. "Trust me, you don't need to hurt yourself to prove a point. My mother has no concept of how spicy her food is to outsiders."

Savita was a beautiful girl, likely in her mid twenties. Zoe had seen many girls of high society over the years, paraded out in their very best dresses, with the most fashionable hairstyles and trends, but Savita put them all to shame. Her features were delicate and pleasant, and her skin a beautiful golden brown. Her thick black hair hung loose, falling forward over her shoulder as she looked down at Simon. She only wore a simple gingham frock, but she could wear a burlap sack and still turn heads. Even her hands were petite and graceful. Then on top of all that, she seemed genuinely kind. She reminded Zoe of something out of a fairy tale —like something ethereal. It was hard to believe a woman like her wasn't already married, even factoring in prejudice against her heritage.

"Thank you," Zoe said with a smile. "But I really did think the flavor was exquisite. Your mother should open a restaurant."

"Don't give her any ideas," muttered Charlie, but his tone was relaxed and with no real malice.

He turned his attention to Zoe, and this time there was a harder edge to his voice. "So, Miss Demas, you are the client I've heard so much about. It's funny, in all these years, you're the first one I've ever seen Quinton bring home for dinner."

Huxley's cheeks flushed, and he swatted at his friend playfully. Zoe understood they were only joking, but she still felt color on her own cheeks.

"Well, Mr. Modi, it is not entirely his fault. I've been told I'm uncommonly stubborn."

Savita chuckled. "What a coincidence, so is Quinton. It's rare to meet someone whose force of will is equal to his."

"Well I expect someone like Ms. Demas doesn't get told no very often."

Zoe held Charlie's gaze evenly. "You'd be surprised."

Quinton cleared his throat. "On that note, I believe we may have outstayed our welcome. Savita, are you sure you're able to care for Simon for a few days, just until we get a few things straightened out?"

She waved him off. "Of course! It's really no trouble."

"I'll compensate you of course."

"Shouldn't that be under Ms. Demas' purview?"

"Charlie, I know it's your natural air, but there's really no need to be an ass all the time," Quinton said with a scowl.

∼

The evening had gone better than Quinton had any right to hope, but he was getting restless. He needed to return Lady Demas to her world before she was noted as missing.

He was getting ready to make their excuses when Charlie caught Quinton's eye and stepped into another room. After a moment, Quinton followed, unsure what to expect.

Charlie silently held out a calling card. Quinton took it and read the name: Zoe Demas. He looked at his friend.

"I asked around like you asked me to, and turns out a small reticule was found near my new business venture. That card was in it."

Quinton knew it wasn't unusual for a maid to carry her ladies' cards with her. Sometimes they paid calls for their ladies, perhaps to a dressmaker, or other service shop, and might need her card to prove who she worked for.

"One of my men asked around and an urchin said he saw Mad Dog with the reticule. My man found him at the Black Goose, as usual, too drunk to walk. I have him sleeping it off in the back room. Thought you might want to talk to him." Charlie paused. "Unless you'd like me to get answers out of him my way."

"No, you don't need to do that." Quinton was all too familiar with Charlie's methods. "I'll speak to him myself, but not tonight. Meet you at the Black Goose tomorrow noon?"

Charlie smiled. "Like old times. We spent many a pay packet there ourselves, back in the day. Maybe John can join and we can throw one back, for old times sake."

Quinton didn't know if Charlie was serious, but it wasn't a bad idea to have a Runner with them, in case anything came of the clue —or in case Charlie's temper got ahead of him again.

"I'll send word to John. Any chance to drink stale ale with old friends." He laughed and Charlie easily joined in.

The two of them rejoined the group, and Quinton quickly made their excuses to Mrs. Modi, whom he called Auntie, and they said goodbye to Simon. Within a few minutes they were on the street and he was hailing for a hackney.

"I apologize for Charlie's rudeness."

"It's not your fault. I'm the one who insisted on coming. And besides, there was no real harm done." Lady Demas smiled.

Quinton sighed. "Perhaps. I do wish he didn't have to pick quite so many fights."

"He's been that way ever since I've known him," Mary chimed in. "Though I've really only known him as an adult and not a wee child."

"It's the same for me, and I've known him for seventeen years."

Lady Demas hesitated for a moment, but apparently decided they were past the distant politeness of strangers. "Do you know why he's so angry?"

"Mm. His father was a British soldier stationed in the Indian colony. He started a family there with his mother, and Charlie and Savita were both born there. When his commission was up, he took his foreign family with him back to England. Charlie was six. That's why Charlie speaks the King's English so well. From what he's willing to talk about, he and his father were quite close—inseparable, even, in the early years. But after a few months back in London, his father's very British parents convinced him to abandon Katy and the kids.

Their relationship wasn't recognized as anything legally binding, so it was easy for him to just...leave."

"That's a sad story."

"It's not uncommon. Charlie never forgave his father, not that I blame him."

"You both don't have a father in your life," commented Lady Demas. "But you are not so angry."

"True. But my father died. Charlie's left by choice. There is a difference. Auntie said once that happy little boy died when his father abandoned them. He was never the same." Quinton paused, shaking his head. "The bastard didn't even have the decency to provide for them financially. He left them destitute. They should have starved, but fortunately Auntie was skilled as a midwife in India, and was able to establish herself and support them. It was an unforgivable act."

There was little to be said to that, so Lady Demas said nothing. The hackney pulled up and Quinton opened the door for them to step up and into it.

She turned back to him. "As for the investigation, what's next, Mr. Huxley?"

"I think we've gotten to know each other

enough after the events of today that you can call me by my Christian name."

"Very well...Quinton." She inclined her head. "Zoe then."

He smiled. "In answer to your question, back to the start. The last place she was seen alive was your aunt's house, so I'm going to start there tomorrow." Quinton paused. "If it's not too much trouble, I could use...an introduction."

Lady Demas—Zoe—grinned. "Pick us up at 2:00 pm, that way we can beat any of the other callers for tea."

"Very well."

Chapter Sixteen

As usual, Quinton was early to the Black Goose. Charlie was right. The three boys had spent many a night there in their youth, drinking more than their fair share of terrible beer. Many of those nights ended in a fight, usually with a fellow drinker, but occasionally between Charlie and himself. John's natural cheerfulness rarely resulted in blows, so he filled the role of peacemaker, even when insults were hurled about the color of his skin by the increasingly drunk clientele. Quinton envied his ability to not take other's talk personally. But he and Charlie were happy to take up the gauntlet if insults continued.

It was here that Charlie lost his eye. It was

many years ago, when they were teenagers. Quinton had started that fight—he'd been drunk, and one of the patrons insulted his mother. They didn't even know his actual mother. It was just one of those things men said to insult each other. It was meant to be generic and harmless. But Quinton had lost his mind. He attacked the other man, not realizing he was one of several dock workers in that night.

The group of laborers were bigger, meaner, and more experienced. As tall as Quinton was, he was still a child in comparison. Charlie had leapt into the fray to defend him. He didn't hesitate. With Quinton's size and Charlie's ruthlessness, they'd held their own for a while. Even John got into that one. But then the knife came out, and in a flash of metal and blood, the deed was done.

The fight broke up quickly after that. No one wanted to be standing around taking responsibility for a maiming like that if a constable showed up. Quinton and John had sobered up fast, thanks to the extra adrenaline and panic. That was the night he met Rory. If he hadn't been there…Quinton still felt guilty about what had happened. Charlie didn't hold it against him—he thought it helped his street credit, but a part of Quinton would always feel like it was his fault.

His thoughts of the past faded as he turned and saw Charlie and John approaching, step in step. They were laughing, but he was too far away to hear what about. Not for the first time, Quinton thought of how these men were his brothers.

"Good morning, Quinton. Ready for a pint already?" John's amiable smile always reached his eyes.

"Business first, pleasure after," replied Quinton. "And this establishment serves pleasure. We should meet for a pint at a place that serves something that doesn't taste like what the night-soil men dispose of."

Charlie laughed. "What this place lacks in refinement is made up for in convenience. It falls under my overlook now."

Quinton nodded as there was truth in that. This part of town was Charlie's—not in an official way that was recognized by any authority, but the people who lived there knew. The betrayal in his formative years, followed by the loss of his eye, galvanized him to be whatever it took to rise above and become a lord unto himself in this little corner of London.

The three of them entered the public house and Charlie led the way to the back room. It took a moment for Quinton's eyes to adjust to the dim interior. He could make out a man laying on the bed, his snores reverberating in the small room. Charlie stalked over, grabbing the man by the back of his shirt and jerking him upright. He woke up with a loud shout, but quieted when he saw the expression on Charlie's face. He swung his feet over the side of the bed.

"I got no beef with you, Charlie. Just mindin' my own, that's it."

All three boys had known Mad Dog since they were boys. He was as much a fixture of the neighborhood as the pub. He looked much the same—still wild-eyed, with unkempt hair and clothes that hadn't seen a bucket of soap since they'd been stitched together.

Charlie held up the reticule and spoke harshly. "Mad Dog, you better be mindin' my own, if you want to walk away. Where did you get this?"

Mad Dog squinted. "I found that bag in tha streets. Had enough in it for the night, it did." He swayed slightly, then continued. "Why you want to know, anyway? I found it myself, fair and square."

John spoke before Charlie could. "The lady who owned the bag found herself dead, that's why. We're a bit interested in who killed her."

The poor drunk's eyes finally opened wide, and he sputtered. "Killed? I didn't killed no one. That bag was in the street, around Princes Street." He squinted again. "Or maybe High Street. I dunno. I already been to Sea Tavern when I stumbled on it."

A sigh escaped Quinton's lips. He hadn't expected much. In all the years he'd known him, he'd never seen Mad Dog wholly sober.

Despite additional questioning, Mad Dog could remember no more. By mutual silent agreement they left the still drunken man to resume his slumber.

The three men took the time to have a pint that tasted of piss, enjoying the nostalgic moment, if not the taste. Although it did not help his investigation, Quinton felt comforted by the three of them tackling the issue together.

"I thought it was a waste of time," Charlie

growled. "I'm not above a good beating but I think Mad Dog has spilled what he has to spill."

John nodded. "It gets us no closer to who killed Lucy, but it was worth the try."

"Agreed." Quinton sighed.

Charlie hesitated, then held out the reticule to Quinton.

"There's nothing inside left, but sometimes ladies like to have a bit of someone they lost. Maybe that snoot nosed friend of yours might like her maid's bag back. Even the toffs have some sentiment."

Quinton took the bag and agreed. "Maybe so."

He took a moment to consult his pocket watch, as always running his finger around the imprinted, yet fading crest as he did so. "But I have more than an hour until I meet with her, and The Crescent Moon has an excellent beef pie. And decent beer."

John clasped his shoulder. "Lead the way."

Chapter Seventeen

"Come along, Mr. Huxley—Quinton." Zoe sauntered along, parasol in hand and cheerful tone to her voice. "If we hurry, we can still make it in time for tea."

Quinton scowled in reply, but he picked up his pace. He knew he was dragging his feet, but this wasn't something he was looking forward to. They were outside his comfort zone and he didn't like it. But it was the last place Lucy was seen alive, and John said she was seen talking to a man.

The trio walked along Piccadilly Street. He and John had shared a hackney to get them both to this part of town where they needed to be after lunch. There were no forgotten souls wasting away in the shadows here, and the filth covering the walkways was significantly less, if not completely absent. Here there were trees and greenery and the air didn't burn his lungs. This area was reserved for the highest members of society.

It wasn't that he couldn't blend with high society. Quinton prided himself on being able to fit into nearly any social group. But high society was one thing—elderly aunts were another. If there was one thing that made him uneasy, it was judgmental old women. But in this case, there was little choice.

Of course they should've been there by now, but Zoe had insisted the hackney drop them off a few blocks away so they could "reflect upon their options in the warm afternoon sun." The girl was truly mad.

Finally their drudge ended. The house Zoe stopped in front of was enormous, much like the other homes in this neighborhood. It was beautiful and ornate and everything that a dowager duchesses' home should be. Quinton's heart sunk.

"You look like you're walking to your own execution," hissed Mary. "Lighten up."

Quinton glared at the girl. He remembered her as a strong-willed and outspoken child, hanging on John's sleeve. Somehow, it was less cute now that she was a young adult, having just passed her eighteenth birthday.

"I don't know if 'lady's maid' is the right calling for someone with your attitude," he hissed back.

Mary grinned. "I don't know. I think me and the lady are getting along just fine."

He couldn't argue with that. The two of them seemed to have developed an uncanny rapport in the short time they'd known each other. It made Quinton suspicious.

"What are you two whispering about?" Zoe didn't wait for an answer. "Come on, I don't want someone else to beat us."

They wouldn't have to rush if she hadn't delayed them with her nonsense, thought Quinton, but he didn't voice his musings out loud. She rushed up the steps of the grand house, with Mary hot on her heels. Quinton was forced to take two steps at a time just to keep up with them.

Zoe's gloved hand reached out and swung the brass knocker back and forth against the door. They didn't have to wait long. A footman, dressed in a red velvet livery, opened the door.

He gave a deferential nod and opened the door to admit them. "Good afternoon, Lady Demas."

"Good afternoon, Thomas," she said, already stripping off her gloves. "Has anyone else arrived yet?"

"Only your cousin, Lord Alexander Dovefield, ma'am."

Zoe audibly groaned. "Aren't we lucky."

As if summoned by the mention of his name, a young man sauntered into the hallway. He was tall—not as tall as Quinton himself, but certainly tall enough to stand out in a crowd—with features that would've been handsome if they weren't so smug. His golden blond hair and gray eyes didn't resemble Zoe's dark curls or piercing blue orbs, but then they wouldn't since they weren't related by blood. From the way his eyes narrowed and his lip curled, Quinton assumed the only blood shared between the two was bad.

"Cousin Zoe." His voice dripped in false sincerity. "How good to see you!"

"Cousin Alexander." Zoe's tone was icy. "I wish the feeling was mutual. Come to bum more money of our rich aunt so your daddy doesn't find out what a pathetic gambler his son is?"

"I think you mean *my* rich aunt." His lips tightened, but the fake smile stayed frozen in place. "Why don't you introduce me to your friends, *Cousin*."

"I'd rather not." Zoe brushed past him as if he were a part of the decor, leaving Mary and Quinton little choice but to follow.

Quinton choked down his laughter and tipped his hat at the seething gentleman as they swept by him. Mary eyed him up and down, but for once her discretion prevailed and she refrained from making any comment.

Of course, he was familiar with Alexander Dovefield, a future baron. They ran in similar circles, but never actually crossed paths. But he knew his reputation—spoiled, arrogant, and vindictive, even by the standards of the *ton*.

An older man, also in a fancy livery and wearing an old-fashioned powdered wig, intercepted them—the butler, Quinton presumed.

"Ms. Demas, you have not been announced!" he exclaimed, the very picture of

British indignation. "Give Jacob your outerwear while Thomas announces you and your...friend?"

"Mr. Huxley." Zoe didn't elaborate further, and the butler was too well trained to ask further questions, though Quinton felt the force of his disapproving glare.

Another footman materialized at his elbow as if out of thin air, causing Quinton to jump. He did a double take, glancing back at Thomas and then Jacob. They were mirror images of the other—twins. He knew posh families preferred footmen of matching height, but to have footmen who were actual twins...that was a sign of the upmost prestige. Even Quinton was impressed.

He swiftly removed his coat and placed it into Jacob's waiting arms. Quinton actually took great pride in his appearance. He knew his clothes weren't the most fashionable or the most expensive, but the fabric was good quality and he made sure they fit well and were in good repair.

"Your maid may wait downstairs," the butler said stiffly.

Zoe and Mary exchanged a meaningful glance. She knew her job. While they were in with the aunt, she would speak with the servants.

"I'll show you into the library." The butler started off toward the closed door, expecting them to follow.

The room they entered was as grand as the outside would lead a person to believe. Books line the walls from floor to ceiling. The floor was red mahogany covered by ornately patterned rugs. Quinton felt his breath catch in his throat. It was the kind of place one might read about in a storybook.

A woman sat in a plush chair, a book sitting in her lap. The passage of time had left its mark upon her, but Quinton wouldn't describe her as elderly. Underneath the fine lines upon her skin, her bone structure was strong and distinctive. Her hair was done up in a loose bun, allowing a few choice silver strands to escape. She wore a day dress that suited her age and status, but was still done in the latest faux-Greek fashion. No one could deny the Dowager Duchess was still a beautiful woman. Quinton didn't miss the gray eyes that evaluated him—the same eyes as her nephew's, but with an intelligence behind them he lacked.

The dowager turned her gaze to her stepniece. "Hmm. A nephew and a niece in one afternoon. I am truly blessed."

Zoe rolled her eyes. "Ugh, don't lump me in with that leech. I assume he was only here to throw away more of your fortune."

"Don't be so harsh, dear. You know how much pressure your cousin is under." The dowager didn't elaborate further—discussing personal family drama in front of a stranger would be in poor taste. "Now what can I help you and your friend with...Mr. Huxley, was it?"

"Your Grace." Quinton bowed respectfully.

The duchess raised her eyebrow. "Well stop hovering and sit down, both of you. You may feel free to poke fun at your cousin, but let's not pretend your visit today is without pretense. Out with it, while Benson fetches us more sandwiches."

Benson acknowledged the request for privacy with a small nod and departed, though Quinton could see the curiosity bursting at the seams of his livery. Only years of rigid discipline kept him from making a comment. Quinton respected it—

he would've been dying to know in his place.

After the door clicked shut, the duchess turned her attention back to them. "Well?"

"I've hired Mr. Huxley to assist me with my inquiries into Lucy's death."

"I see...and Mr. Huxley, what exactly is your job description that makes you qualified to assist my niece? Are you an investigator or a constable of some kind?"

"I act as a neutral party and mediator in various delicate situations."

"Ah, so a thief-taker."

"No, not a thief-taker," Quinton said quickly.

Thief-takers had a long history in England as individuals hired to capture criminals and negotiate the return of stolen goods. Once they had been looked at as a necessary, even important, part of the justice system, but public opinion had turned against them in recent years. Now of days the words were practically synonymous with corruption.

"Uh huh." The dowager didn't look convinced. "But your services that my niece has engaged...they involve tracking down a criminal?"

"Um, well, yes. I suppose that is one way of phrasing things." Quinton shifted in his plush chair—it was so soft it felt as though it was swallowing him.

"So the services you provide are thief-taker...adjacent?" The older woman's eyes sparkled.

"Aunt Theo, stop." Zoe finally interrupted the interrogation. "We've uncovered some sensitive information about Lucy and we think it may be related to a member of your staff."

"Very well, if you insist. Pour some tea for your guest, dear."

Zoe sighed dramatically, but didn't let the act of serving tea stop her from talking. "We found out that Lucy was afraid of someone—Mr. Huxley, this is sugar free house, but would you like any honey or cream?"

"Uh, yes, please."

"Right." She dumped the sweetener and cream in the cup and handed it to him. He snatched a cucumber sandwich and took a sip of the warm beverage as she continued her monologue. "

Quinton took another sip of his sweet beverage to hide his lips quirking up at the corners. He'd never had tea with honey, but he was not upset about the flavor. Many women had taken up the cause of abolition by boycotting sugar two years ago, one of the main products produced by slaves. But most had given up when slavery was made illegal in London. Of course, the many footholds of the British empire beyond its own shores were left untouched by the new law. He was impressed the duchess was still keeping up with the cause.

When Zoe finished her explanation, the duchess placed her saucer on the table beside her chair. "Well I can honestly say I wasn't expecting you to say any of that. Although I would be very disturbed to find out that any man in this house would be so rude to a woman. You don't think it's connected to this business in her past, do you?"

Just then the butler returned, the platter of anticipated sandwiches in his hand. Quinton eyed them like a lion eyed a mouse—he didn't know why rich people insisted on making delicious food in tiny portions. Even with the lunch at the Crescent Moon he felt ravenous.

The conversation died; there was no way

to make something seem more suspicious than to stop talking as soon as someone entered the room. But Quinton's stomach was rumbling too much for him to come up with a clever decoy topic.

"It's not impossible. We still don't know who fathered her son. I'd like to talk to your footmen and see what the confrontation was about." Quinton popped another sandwich in his mouth.

"Very well." Theo turned back to the butler. "Please have Thomas and Jacob come in."

The man did as asked and soon produced the twins. Neither looked very comfortable at having been summoned. Quinton took a moment to assess their appearance—they were tall and lanky, with brownish hair and dark eyes. Neither resembled the ruddy faced and redheaded Simon. But the qualities children took from their parents were often difficult to predict.

Quinton spoke quickly. "I understand one of you spoke to Lucy on the day she picked up the flier."

He hadn't asked a question, but the implication was obvious. He was waiting for one of them to volunteer the information.

It took a moment, but finally Jacob spoke. "Yes sir, I did speak with her before she left."

Finally. "What about?"

Jacob shifted from foot to foot and kept his eyes on the rug.

"You aren't in trouble, Jacob, but it's very important you are honest," said the dowager ominously.

The boy sighed. "I asked her where she was headed after this...you know, like what was she planning on doing on her day off? But I was surprised by what she said."

"And what was that?" Zoe's voice was strained; Quinton could tell she was growing impatient.

Jacob hesitated before finally saying, "Westminster Pit."

Even Quinton was surprised by that. "What?"

"I told her that was no place for a respectable woman, especially by herself." Now that the secret had been spoken, the boy seemed to gush with words. "She said she had to go, that it was important. She was meeting someone and she didn't want to miss it. I even offered to go with her, after work, but she said she couldn't wait. Had to be there at 4:00."

The dowager raised a hand, stopping the torrent. "It's alright, Jacob. We know you weren't doing anything wrong."

"Yes, thank you for telling us, Jacob," said Quinton to reassure the boy. "But she didn't say who she was meeting?"

He shook his head. "No."

"Hmm. And how did you know Lucy? Were you friends, or...?"

"We were on friendly terms." Jacob's face turned a shade of red. "In truth, I would've liked to have known her better. She seemed like a right nice girl. But she didn't want anything other than friendship from me."

Quinton thought it unlikely he was the criminal mastermind they were after. "Very well. You may go."

Both boys exited the room as fast as decorum allowed. Quinton didn't blame them.

Zoe's brow furrowed. "Westminster Pit? That doesn't sound like somewhere Lucy would go."

"No, it does not. But it does explain the torn note. Which means something very unusual must've happened to make her alter her behavior and ignore her natural instincts to such an extreme degree." Quinton mulled this new information over in his mind. At least it was something—a thread that could be pulled on. All he could hope is it would lead them to their next thread.

"Well that was very exciting." The dowager eyed Quinton again, a glint in her eye. "I'm curious, do thief-takers get the reward from the government as well as private payment in circumstances such as these?"

"Aunt Theo!" exclaimed Zoe.

Quinton snorted, nearly choking on his last sip of tea. The old dragon didn't pull any punches. "I wonder if I've done something to offend you, Your Grace?"

"On the contrary." Her eyes hadn't lost their glint. "I find this whole thing very intriguing."

Zoe scolded her aunt, and Quinton pulled his familiar pocket watch from his coat pocket. If they hurried, they could still make it. "If you will excuse me, I have another appointment I should be getting to."

"Where did you get that?"

Quinton blinked. "What?"

"The pocket watch." The dowager's eyes

were locked on the object. "Where did you get it?"

"Oh. It was my father's. My mother gave it to me." Quinton cleared his throat and placed it back in his pocket. He wasn't sure why she was suddenly so intrigued by the watch, but something about her intense interest made him uncomfortable.

"The symbol on it...may I see it?"

Quinton glanced at Zoe, seeking direction. She just shrugged her shoulders, which was less than helpful. He hesitated, but he didn't want to offend Zoe's beloved aunt, even if she was eccentric. He rose and walked over to place the golden ornament in her outstretched palm.

He knew the symbol she was speaking about. It was etched into the gold—over the years he had rubbed his thumb across its surface so much that it was nearly worn away, but the outline was still visible. It was a shield, with a bear on one side and a lion on the other, and a crown at the top.

The duchess inspected it, rubbing her own fingers lightly across its surface. When she spoke, it seemed to be for her own benefit.

"Mm. It reminds me of something from...a long time ago."

Quinton took the watch back and slipped it back in his pocket. "Thank you for your hospitality, Your Grace. Good afternoon."

"I need to go too, Aunt Theo. But thanks for your help." Zoe gave her aunt a peck on the cheek and followed Quinton out of the room.

"What was that about?" he hissed as soon as the door closed behind them.

"I don't know. It's probably nothing. Let's get Mary."

The other footman—Thomas—fetched Mary, and the three of them made their escape. Quinton breathed a sigh of relief as soon as the fresh air hit his face, as Zoe quickly filled Mary in on what they'd learned from Jacob.

"Well what now, *thief-taker?*" said Zoe with a devilish smile.

Quinton ignored her. "Mary, how did you get on downstairs? Did the other maids have anything to say about Lucy?"

"Nothing as useful as that, but one of the parlor maids did remember speaking with her that day. Lucy didn't tell her where she was going, but she did say she had an appointment. The maid said she seemed nervous, but not particularly frightened. In fact, she said if she didn't know better she might think she was excited."

"Interesting," murmured Quinton.

"Very. But like I asked before, where are we going now?" This time Zoe's voice was tinged with annoyance.

"I am going to Westminster Pit," said Quinton with a grumble. "You are going home."

Chapter Eighteen

The smell of blood and body odor hit Zoe like a ton of bricks. She wrinkled her nose and held up a handkerchief laced with lavender, trying to block the atrocious scent.

The roar from the crowd within the building could be heard from the street outside. Inside it was nearly deafening. People of all walks of life were pressed together in the throng—laborers, servants, merchants, and even gentleman—anyone who had coin to spare, and many who didn't.

Of course the women were few and far between, and none were ladies. Zoe pulled the hood of her cloak down lower over her face. Much as she might scorn the rules of society, the last thing she needed was to be recognized here.

Mary was on one side of her, arm in arm. She clearly had more experience at events like this; she used her free arm to push and shove and elbow her way through the crowd, pulling Zoe along.

Quinton was on her other side, and though he wasn't touching her, Zoe could feel the angry energy radiating off him. He hadn't wanted her to come here—in fact he had insisted she and Mary go home while he handle this. She had insisted just as strongly that they had every right to come along. In the fight that ensued, many things were said, none of them particularly kind.

Despite his objections, there actually wasn't much he could do to stop her, short of dragging her home by her hair—and though he threatened to do it, Zoe had been fairly confident he wouldn't follow through. In truth, he'd always been surprisingly good natured about her demands. He might grumble and moan, but he would usually let her have her way. But this was the first time she'd seen him genuinely angry. Unfortunately for him, it was not in her nature to acquiesce.

After the tense standoff, the moment finally passed, and he had accepted the reality that she would be there whether or not he liked it. He didn't like it, but there wasn't much Zoe could do about that. Everyone had to do things they didn't like sometimes.

As they got closer, the sound of animals screeching and yipping became louder than the sound of the people jeering. Quinton veered, guiding them up a set of stairs to the balcony. The throng pressed her against the balcony until Quinton growled and moved his bulk in between her and them. Until that point, she'd been too jostled about and eager to really take stock of the actual entertainment being presented. Now she could focus on nothing else.

Of course she was aware of the concept of bull baiting—she didn't live in a bubble. They said letting the dogs work the bull out made the meat more tender. She ate meat; she knew where it came from. But nothing could have prepared her for the brutality of seeing it live.

The bull was staked in the middle of the pit, but it didn't really matter whether or not it was tied. The great beast was still alive, but only just. Blood oozed from gashes on his face and throat and legs as he lay there in the dirt, gasping for breath.

Beside the bull lay the creature responsible for its fate. The dog was a beast unto itself—it was huge, like a wolf out of a haunting fairy tale. Its head alone was as big as a serving platter, with a square face and bulging eyes. It was built like a brick, muscular and stocky. Its black coat hid some of the blood, but its red life force also stained the dirt.

It whined, trying to drag itself toward a man at the end of the pit. Zoe assumed it was its master. The tone of the crowd expressed no sympathy for either creature, only disappointment that the fight hadn't lasted longer. Bile rose in her throat and she gripped the rail to steady herself.

It wasn't the first time she had been amid a crowd baying for blood. The sensations were all too familiar; the press of bodies, the smell of blood mixing with earth, and the roar of a mass of people who no longer functioned as individuals, but as a single, monstrous entity with only one goal—suffering and death. Zoe felt as though she was seven years old again, glimpsing the carnage through the crowd, recoiling in horror as she watched a severed head roll off the platform, landing in the slick street with a sickening squelch.

A firm hand gripping her forearm brought Zoe crashing back to reality. She wasn't a helpless child anymore, and this wasn't France. She let out a shuddering breath and glanced over to see Quinton's hand still resting on her arm. When he saw her looking he quickly pulled it away. Zoe swallowed hard and turned her attention away from the spectacle.

"There!" Quinton pointed to a burly man collecting bets near the front of the pit. "Perhaps he might remember Lucy."

The three of them turned as one and made their way to the man, Quinton and Mary still instinctively keeping Zoe in the middle. The crowd ebbed and flowed as boos and hissing were sent in the direction of the arena, but finally they were at the man's side.

"Excuse me," Quinton bellowed in the man's ear. "Got a question for you."

As the huge man turned, Zoe saw the right side of his face was marred by several crisscrossing scars. But the eyes regarding them were surprisingly intelligent, and he nodded at Quinton.

Zoe took out her most recent sketch of Lucy, drawn from the recesses of her guilty memories, and handed it to the man.

Quinton asked, "Did you see this woman a few days ago? We think she may have been here."

The man took the sketch, examining it carefully, then glanced behind Zoe. His hand shot out to grab the collar of a scrawny man.

"You're not running out on me, Danny!" He shoved the other man backwards as if he were a sack of potatoes. "I got that IOU in my pocket, and you'll pay up 'fore you leave, or I'll put the hurt on you like you wouldn't believe!"

The delinquent Danny pouted, sputtering excuses, but the big man just held up a hand to stop his yammering. "I'll deal with the likes of you in a minute. I'm talkin' to tha lady now."

He handed the sketch back to Zoe. "I seen her. She was 'ere alone, then she met up with a man. Weren't too keen on him at first, but after some discussion she up and left with him. I remember her on account of she smiled at me, nice like. I could tell she was a nice lady and not the type for this crowd—like yourself, ma'am."

Quinton grabbed his arm as he was turning to leave. "Wait. Do you remember what this man looked like?"

The big man paused, his face twisted in the effort of recollection. "Weren't nothin' particular 'bout 'im. Dressed nice. No scars. All his teeth."

She shared a glance with Quinton. There wasn't anything else to be learned from the avenue.

"Thank you very much, sir, for your help."

He smiled, showing at least three missing teeth. "Not many folks 'round 'ere call me 'sir.'"

Zoe smiled back. His attention was taken with Danny and those like him, while she and her companions regrouped. In a moment of morbid curiosity, she glanced back at the arena.

She saw the bull had been hauled away, leaving a bloody trail, but the dog was still there. A man stood above it, a club in hand and a foot on the beast's throat.

Her actions after that were without

thought—primal instincts taking over her powers of reason. She slipped between the rope barricades and hurled the full force of her body at the man. Though she was tall for a woman, her weight was still only a fraction of his, but she had surprise and momentum on her side. They crashed into the dirt, his body absorbing most of the impact.

She scrambled for the club with single-mindedly viciousness while her victim cursed and thrashed at her. A force suddenly yanked her backwards. She dangled in the air, suspended from Quinton's outstretched arm.

"My god, woman, what has possessed you?"

"He was going to kill the dog!"

"What does that have to do with you behaving like a mad woman?!" Quinton sighed and placed her back on the ground. "I know it's brutal, but the beast is badly wounded. A quick death would be a kindness."

By this point the man had managed to stand. He opened his mouth to say something, but a glare from Quinton shut his mouth. "I realize you may feel like the aggrieved party here, but I have very little sympathy for anyone who would subject an animal to this fate. I suggest you console yourself with the fact it was the lady who bowled you over, and not I."

Tears fill her eyes, much to her chagrin. "It's not fair. It's not the dog's fault. He's just doing what he's trained to do and they're gonna throw him away like trash."

His expression softened, and he looked down at the poor creature. He sighed again, this time with his whole body. Zoe pinpointed that as the exact moment when he came over to her side.

"How much for the dog?"

The owner blinked. "What? It's half dead already. It's worthless."

"So any money you make off the beast is a boon to you." Quinton pulled a pocket-book out and pulled out some cash. "I'll give you five pounds for it."

His eyes widened, but then immediately narrowed as he realized a deal could be made. "Ten pound."

"Six."

"Eight."

"Seven, and that's as high as I'll go."

"Done."

Quinton transferred the cash and turned

his body to exclude the man, clearly signally that he was dismissed. Zoe thought how well he would fit in among the aristocrats.

"Well, now you own a dog—half a dog, at least." Mary crossed her arms and bit her lower lip. "Your mother will be thrilled."

The reality of what she had done dawned on Zoe. The dog wasn't in good shape; he looked up at her with big brown eyes, but his body was wet with blood and his back leg lay twisted at an unnatural angle. She swallowed hard and covered her mouth with her hand.

"Don't lose your nerve on me now...Zoe. I can't guarantee that the beast will live, but we'll give it our best shot. Rory doesn't just know about human anatomy; he's looked after my Oscar for years. I'll take the beast there tonight and let you know tomorrow what can be done." Quinton scooped the dog up effortlessly; it whimpered but did little beyond that.

Zoe smiled. "Thank you, Mr. Huxley. I very much appreciate this. I will pay you back the seven pounds as well."

"I'll put it on your tab."

Chapter Nineteen

The loud thumps of Quinton's boot slamming against the wooden door echoed down the dark street. Everything was quiet at this time of night, so the sound seemed deafeningly loud.

Rory lived in a shockingly upscale part of London. It wasn't all that far from where the Dovefield's resided, his townhome tucked away off on a side street, in between a dentist and a doctor. They hated the uneducated Scotsman who had taken up residence in their midst, but money spoke louder than bloodlines these days.

He heard rumblings from inside the house, and as they got closer, he could make out the distinct sound of cursing through a thicker than usual Scottish accent. The door opened inwards, slamming against the wall.

"Do ya have any idea wat time a night 'tis?" hissed Rory.

"Trust me, I am very aware."

Rory sighed and pushed some of his reddish blond hair out of his eyes. He looked Quinton up and down, taking in the blood smeared clothes, the bags under the eyes, the mud on his boots, and finally the enormous bleeding dog in his arms.

"What on God's green earth is going on?" This time the accent was less pronounced.

"Look, it's been a long night. Are you going to help me with this or not?"

The door opened wider. "Get in here before you wake up all the neighbors."

Quinton entered, his arms sore from the weight of the beast. Rory pushed past him, still rubbing the sleep from his eyes. He gestured vaguely. "Bring it out back."

There was an outbuilding in his garden that Rory had revamped for purposes such as these. Quinton carried the dog inside and laid it out on the stained butcher block. Rory kept the space impeccably clean, so much so that the faint scent of lye lingered in the air, but nothing could completely cover the staining of blood or the persistent scent of decay.

Quinton was surprised at how little the creature had whined. Instead it just lay there, silently staring at him with its big brown eyes.

He absently patted its sticky head. "Good boy."

The events of the evening suddenly caught up with him all at once, exhaustion overcoming him. Quinton let out a deep breath, slumping against the wall.

"Go pour yourself a drink and sit on the couch. It'll take me a minute to evaluate the damage, and I don't need to add stitching you up after you inevitably fall asleep standing there and crack your head open to my late night workload."

"I'm too tired this time to argue with you."

Quinton went into the sitting room and poured himself a hefty draught of the scotch whiskey Rory loved so much. It tasted like a campfire in his mouth, swirling with heat and smoke. Quinton appreciated the refined experience, but the truth was he preferred the smooth taste of Irish or English whiskey. Not that he would ever admit it to Rory—for him, scotch was the sacred epitome of all beverages.

Rory had done well for himself as a resurrectionist. It was a lucrative trade, and Rory was one of the best. His home was modest by the standards of upper society, but a mansion compared to the masses of Londoners living in squalid, cramped tenements. Even those who had gainful employment often lived on their employer's property, often in their employer's own home. Rory had carved out a niche for himself in the world—not quite a lord, not quite a servant, not quite a merchant, not quite a tradesman. Quinton didn't know where exactly Rory fit in the social hierarchy, but he had to admit, even he didn't have a proper sitting room.

He was dozing off when Rory finally reentered the room, wiping the blood from his hands with a damp cloth. He poured himself his own heavy draught.

"You know, you could've cleaned up a little while you were waiting."

"The thought honestly never occurred to me." Quinton took another sip. "Will the creature live?"

"Indeed. Most of the damage was superficial, except for a few fractured ribs and a broken back leg. If I can keep the leg stable, he should be back in fighting form in a couple of months." Rory let out a deep breath and collapsed into the chair across from him. "So are you going to tell me the story?"

It didn't take as long as Quinton thought it would to summarize the evening's events. Rory sat there the whole time, sipping his scotch and quietly listening.

When Quinton was finished, he was silent. After a few moments he finally said, "I knew you liked her, but I didn't think you were that far gone."

"What are you talking about?"

"You're including her in your investigation. You took her to a bull baiting fight, despite your better judgment. Then you bought her pet—if you can call that thing in there a pet." Rory chuckled. "She's got you wrapped around her finger."

"You're talking nonsense, as usual. I have done all in my power to exclude her. She is simply uncontrollable."

"My good man, you are in my home doing her a favor at this unholy hour. It's not the kind of thing one does for casual acquaintances. It seems uncontrollable is your type."

"Whatever you say, Rory." Quinton rolled his eyes. "Even if it were true, which it isn't, it doesn't matter. She's a gentlewoman, and I'm just...me. There's no world where anything more could happen."

"*Love looks not with the eyes, but with the mind, and therefore is winged Cupid painted blind.*"

"Rory, I'm too tired for this. Speak plainly if you must speak."

"Fine. Feelings aren't rational. You may know logically that nothing can come of it, but love isn't logical. The heart is often blind in these matters." Rory shrugged and settled back into his chair. "And you might consider saying thank you instead of biting my head off, since you in fact came to me with this very inconvenient and ill-timed favor."

Quinton's cheeks flushed. "I'm sorry. Thank you, Rory, I mean it. You've always come through for me and you're right, I have no right to snap at you."

Rory waved a dismissive hand. "It's forgotten. Just remember that denial will bring more harm than good in the long run."

In truth, Rory's observation had struck a nerve that Quinton hadn't realized was there. "Even if what you've said is true, which I'm not saying it is, then what does it matter? She's supposed to end up some rich lord's wife, attending balls and calling on the wives of all the other rich lords. I'm just a detour in a life that's already set in stone."

"That girl's destiny was to marry a French aristocrat and become an ornament in a palace. Then her destiny was to die in the street like the rest of her kind. You may think her life is set in stone, but she has already cheated fate more times than most."

"I hadn't considered it in that light. But it doesn't change the fact that no matter where she ends up, she's still a lady and I'm still the son of an actress."

"You don't give her enough credit. She's beautiful and rich and blue blooded, aye, but not every rich, beautiful, high-born girl would care how her maid died, or hire an investigator to solve her death, or stand in the room with a 'grave robber' discussing Shakespeare. There's more depth to that lady than meets the eye."

"So people keep saying," said Quinton with a sigh. "But it's irrelevant. Even if she was willing to sacrifice everything for someone like me, I would never let her. The scandal would destroy her."

Rory raised his hands in surrender. "Fine, have it your way. My last word of advice for the evening is don't EVER tell a woman that her feelings are irrelevant." He glanced toward the back door. "So what do you want to do about the dog?"

Quinton had honestly forgotten about the dog. "Um, can I leave him here for a couple days? I'll discuss it with Zoe—Lady Demas and make some arrangements to collect him as soon as possible. She'll pay for your services as well, of course."

"Very well. I should probably keep an eye on him anyway to make sure there isn't anything I've missed." Rory cleared his throat. "Do you want me to take care of...the other thing?"

The heat returned to Quinton's cheeks. "Um, yes, I suppose so."

Rory laughed. "I don't know why you get so uncomfortable about it. An animal doesn't know any better. He doesn't need his bollocks if fate has determined he will live in a house."

"Yes of course. Naturally. Anyhow, I should get going."

"At this hour you might as well not even go to bed."

"Nevertheless I think I will." Quinton stood up. "Thank you, Rory, genuinely. I owe you one."

Rory also rose to his feet. "I won't disagree with you on that front."

Chapter Twenty

Exhaustion took its toll; Zoe dosed off twice in the hackney on the way home, but roused herself as they neared the house. It had been a long day. She could think of nothing but a warm bath to wash the stench of the crowd from her, followed by the embrace of a soft pillow.

It became apparent as soon as she and Mary crossed the threshold that her fantasy would not be happening soon.

Quaid spoke before she did. "Lady Zoe, your mother would like to see you in her sitting room."

Though Zoe often thought of their butler as ancient, in truth, he was still south of seventy, and still stood ramrod straight. He put on a very stuffy and traditional air, but was actually an intelligent and loyal man. He'd been with Hugh Dovefield since before his first wife died, and always had a particular fondness for Zoe.

The butler leaned forward, lowering his voice. "She has been waiting for some time, and does not appear happy."

"Well I suppose this conversation was inevitable." Zoe sighed. "Thank you, Quaid."

With a slight nod, he stepped aside, his job done for the time being. His gaze changed as his eyes found Mary. It appeared she was not yet forgiven for her ghost impersonation. She for once kept her eyes down and said nothing.

Zoe sighed again, thinking of her waiting mother. She left early with Mary, been gone all day, and had neglected to leave as much as a note. This conversation was indeed inevitable. She would be in for a tongue lashing.

"Go to bed Mary. I'll change myself tonight—it's going to be a while."

Mary didn't argue—the day had been just as long for her. She said goodnight, and Zoe went to her mother's sitting room. It was a cheerful room, painted in a warm pastel yellow and decorated in a charming, feminine style. However, the woman waiting was anything but cheerful at the moment.

Zoe closed the door behind her, trying to come up with a strategy for war. Perhaps she could ward off the worst of it with a preemptive strike.

"I should have let you know where I was, *mama*. I'm sorry. Please don't be angry."

Simone was silent for a moment, anger radiating from her. When she spoke, her tone was ice cold.

"I am beyond angry Zoe. And absolutely beyond comprehension. You allowed Hugh and I to worry all day as to your whereabouts, and this evening you did not bother to even show up for dinner with the Livingstons. We had to make up a lie that you were in bed with a migraine, which I could tell Margret did not believe, by the way. And then, this evening, we were told you visited Theodosia with a man—a stranger—asking about Lucy. It's bad enough you don't care about your own reputation, but you clearly have absolutely no interest in how your eccentric behavior affects ours." With each word, the anger in Simone's voice deepened until by the end she could barely speak.

So much for her preemptive strike. That little rotter Alexander, thought Zoe. Who else would bother to make trouble for her? It was a blessing the bull baiting plans were made outside the house. And the brute of a dog! At least she didn't have to explain that tonight. That was an argument for another time.

"I don't need permission to see my Aunt. What we spoke of is a private matter, unless Theo chooses to share. Otherwise it is simply gossip. A bit below you, isn't it mama?"

Even as she spoke, she knew it was the wrong move. It would make Simone even angrier. But where she and her mother were concerned, Zoe was skilled at winning battles, but always lost the war.

It didn't seem possible, but Simone's voice became even icier. "Do you not remember where we came from, Zoe? You have no idea what I sacrificed—what I had to do to get us out of France, not to mention keeping us alive after. Hugh Dovefield was a windfall beyond anything we could've hoped for, but I don't expect he knew his French stepdaughter would bring ruin to his reputation."

"His reputation, *mama*? Hugh's reputation? Let's be honest. This is not about Hugh. It's your reputation you are protecting—after all, it's always been the most important thing to you, even more important than me." Zoe blinked back the tears threatening to fall. "I do remember—I remember how you got us out. I'll never be free of those memories. But you know what else I remember? You left *papa* to die."

Simone recoiled as if struck. "Your *papa*? I begged your *papa* to leave when we had the chance. He refused to acknowledge the danger, always ready to believe the best of his friends—always believing that things would just...work out for him. He died because he was a foolish man with a fool's reasoning. His death is on him. Your life is on me."

Zoe's fatigue had been forgotten in the heat of battle, but it suddenly returned with a vengeance. Her legs were like jelly. Somehow, their worst arguments always circled back around to the same thing.

She settled heavily into the sofa near the fireplace. As she leaned back, the tears she'd been holding back finally slid past her closed eyes. It didn't take long before she felt her mother's weight on the cushion next to her. A feeling of warmth filled her as Zoe's head rested against her mother's shoulder. Simone slid her arms around her daughter and a silence weighted the room.

"I still miss him, *mama*," said Zoe finally. "I miss the way he laughed when he picked me up. I miss the sound of his voice. I miss the way he held me. I miss the way he loved me."

Simone's voice was even, but Zoe could hear the sadness behind it. "Believe it or not, I miss him too sometimes. I miss his sense of humor. He could find the humor in everything. He thought you were the most wonderful thing in the world. It was one thing we actually agreed on. He loved to make you laugh."

Zoe smiled through her tears. "I hardly remember a time when he was with me that I didn't laugh."

Both women were quiet for a moment.

"I haven't heard you laugh enough lately, *chaton*." Simone paused, then started to sing softly in French. "*Ah! Vous Dirai-je mama, Ce qui cause mon torment.*"

Zoe sighed, then smiled at the childhood nursery rhyme. *Shall I tell you my torment, mama?* She well remembered singing the rhyme growing up in France. *Kitten.* Her mother had not called her that for some time, an endearment from her childhood.

"I haven't found my way in this world, *mama*, not like you. I haven't found a place I belong. I love things here, yes. You, Hugh, my art, *les petits* of course." She paused, then sat up and met her mother's eyes. "I am grateful, *mama*, for what you did in France. I know you saved our lives. I know it was difficult. Your way is not my way. I need to find my way myself."

Simone was quiet, but met Zoe's eyes. The silence stretched on as she waited.

"There was a child. Of Lucy's." Zoe's tone was flat; she'd used up her tears.

Simone straightened up. "A child? Lucy had a child?"

Zoe told her mother of the trip to the baby farm, of buying a toddler, and of the children they left behind. "The woman said the women were of poor moral caliber, but that wasn't true of Lucy and I doubt it's true of the other mothers. They just didn't have a choice. You know how hard it is for a mother with no husband to care for themselves and their children."

"No, you are right. It is difficult." Simone spoke softly, her eyes distant.

It hadn't escaped Zoe that her mother had once been in a similar position. When they first arrived in London, she was old enough to not need constant care, but the adjustment had still been a struggle for both of them. For the first time, Zoe realized how difficult it must have been for her mother, alone in a foreign country, with a daughter to protect. She felt a sudden rush of shame at how she had treated her mother. Zoe leaned back into her mother, unable to put into words her changing view of the world. She was grateful when her mother changed the subject.

"Where is Lucy's child now?"

Zoe hesitated, knowing her travels to London's east-end would not be well received. She chose her words carefully.

"The man I hired to investigate, a Mr. Huxley, knew of a woman who would care for the boy. We agreed I would pay for his care. But he is safe now."

"Good. I am glad Lucy's babe is safe." Simone gazed into the flickering flames of the fireplace. "My situation is long removed from the mother's needing baby farms. I have resources now. And *les petits* are older, needing me less as they are more involved in schooling." She wrapped her arms tighter around Zoe. "Sometimes I forget you are changing, *chaton*—growing up. Perhaps I need to find a way to change as well. This path you are following. You cannot let it go? Let your investigator man do his job?"

Zoe said nothing for a moment. "I am not sure myself, *mama*, but this is giving me purpose. For the first time in my life, I feel as though my actions have…meaning. I need to see where it leads, and perhaps who I am at the end. I cannot explain it beyond that."

"Well I cannot pretend I understand. But I will try. I do think you should be careful about your association with this man. I do not say this to provoke you—I simply want what is best for you."

"Thank you, *mama*." Zoe kissed her mother's cheek, ignoring the latter part of her statement. "It was wrong of me to leave no word on where I was all day. I am truly sorry for the worry you spent because of me."

Simone smiled. "It was all I thought of for

years, keeping you safe. I know it's not the same now, but I will always worry about you, *chaton*. Always."

Zoe realized again how true that was.

"I can't promise I will tell you my every move, mama. But I won't let you worry like today again. *D'accord?*"

"I will take what you will give, Zoe. Agreed."

∽

The next morning Zoe's head throbbed as she made her way to the breakfast room. She wasn't prone to the migraines that plagued others, but the lack of sleep and abundance of tears definitely gave her a headache. Coffee might help.

She heard voices as she approached the dining room, followed by a low laugh. Her pace slowed as she wondered who would be visiting with Hugh at such an hour. She almost went back to her room for a while rather than submit her headache to a stranger. But the desire for coffee won out, and she bravely entered the dining room. To her delight, it was not a stranger, but Hugh's good friend and fellow barrister, William Garrow, who sat across from him. He rose when he caught sight of Zoe.

"*Mon cherie.* You are more beautiful each time I see you!" Garrow was no more French than the prince himself, but he always fondly called Zoe by the French endearment of affection. "It does an old man's heart good to see you prospering."

Zoe laughed. She was always glad to see Mr. Garrow, as he was not only fond of Zoe but a fascinating person himself.

"You have always made liberal use of Spanish coin, Mr. Garrow, though you are hardly old. But I am pleased to see you today. A legal case, no doubt?"

A look passed between the men, but before Zoe guessed at its meaning, Hugh spoke.

"Yes, a case. Something thorny, I'm afraid."

Zoe helped herself to coffee from the sideboard and Hugh signaled the footman for a fresh pot. She sat next to Hugh and across from Garrow, and he chatted with her about mundane things.

"How is Eliza, Mr. Garrow? I simply do

not travel in the same circles since her marriage to Mr. Lettsom."

As a close friend of Hugh's, Mr. Garrow had been a part of Zoe's life even before the wedding. His daughter Eliza was a few years older than Zoe and their paths had crossed often.

"She is well, Zoe. I don't see her myself often enough. I just don't have the energy for a great deal beyond work these days." The words were spoken in a matter-of-fact way, but Zoe could feel the sadness behind them. Mr. Garrow's beloved wife, Sarah, had died one year previously, and he had yet to recover.

Her parents were very close mouth about it, but Zoe had pieced together through the years that the Garrow's relationship had been an unconventional one. They were together a long time without a wedding, with both their children born years before wedlock. Most wouldn't have recovered from the scandal, but they simply pretended there was no scandal. The even more shocking thing is that it worked.

Hugh rose to help himself to the shirred eggs and spoke casually. "I was telling

William of the loss of Lucy. And your continued...interest...in her."

Zoe stopped mid sip, contemplating her stepfather. Then she shrugged and nodded. "I am interested in justice, father. I suspect Mr. Garrow is the wrong one to argue against that."

Garrow laughed, the clouds of his grief parting briefly. "Well played, mon cherie, well played."

Early in his career as a barrister, William Garrow blazed a trail of revolutionary justice, while also leaving many bridges burning in the flames. He was the first to suggest that all people should be given a defense, and that everyone accused of a crime should be considered innocent until proven guilty. It was not a popular opinion in every circle, but it established him quickly in the world of law and order.

It was during this period in his life that he and Hugh became friends, as Garrow preached sentiments Hugh already believed in. Their bond had endured many years now, despite Garrow being a decade his junior. His passionate character had brought him farther than Hugh's content temperament, even all the way to Parliament. Although his first passion would always be for the law, his deepest enjoyment came from spirited debate, so he did well in politics.

Zoe elaborated for his benefit. "Lucy was my maid, and has no family we are aware of. Justice should not begin and end with payment for a burial."

Hugh answered. "But trouble should not be sought when none exists. Lucy met with a tragic accident, Zoe. It is unfair, but there is no real justice to be sought."

She debated how much to reveal to her father about what she'd already uncovered. "But it is not as tidy as you would imply—there are questions. So what harm can come from looking a little closer? If there is nothing to be found, then nothing will be found. There is no loss of anything but my time." She paused for dramatic effect, holding Hugh's gaze. "But if we do nothing, and there is a person who holds responsibility, the stakes are much higher. Then justice is not served, not for Lucy. And if a person can help justice be found, and chooses not to, then perhaps a bit of the blood is on their hands as well. Not the blood of the crime, but the blood of justice, who dies as well."

A silence filled the room, and for a long moment no one spoke.

"If only there was a place for women in the court, my dear. Not only can you debate with the best of them, but your natural flair for the dramatic would guarantee you a spotlight. That's how I did it." William Garrow leaned back in his chair and smiled. "Well played, little one, well played."

Zoe gave a faux bow, secretly thrilled at the praise.

Garrow laughed, then changed the subject.

"Tell me, mon cherie, if a man steals his employer's silver, and is caught, what are the legal steps for justice?"

Leaning back in her chair and crossing her arms, Zoe smiled. Garrow had started this game when she was a child, asking legal questions to keep her interest when she became bored. She answered easily.

"It depends on the definition of justice, Mr. Garrow. If an employer wishes for legal justice, he will call a magistrate and file charges. But he must be prepared to follow through himself, as he will likely have to present evidence both to the grand jury and again at trial. It is a bit of work, and many simply don't want to pursue justice in that way. If you are wealthy of course you can hire someone like my stepfather to do the work."

"Very good. What is the other alternative?"

"Or the employer can simply discharge the man with no reference, and call the matter done." Zoe stopped to think. "Or.... perhaps the employer could question why a man that works for him would want to steal his silver. The full story often clarifies the next step."

Garrow threw back his head and laughed again. "You will find your way, mon cherie." He glanced at Hugh. "She will make you proud, my friend."

Hugh said nothing, but his expression softened. He sighed after a moment and walked to the door. Garrow followed, pausing at the door to look back at Zoe with a cheeky wink. Zoe wasn't sure what had changed, but she felt a shift between her and Hugh. Perhaps a bit of respect had been earned.

Chapter Twenty-One

"My, my, two visits in as many days." Theo laughed and gestured for Zoe to sit down. "Without your handsome new friend this time?"

"No, not this time." Zoe let herself collapse onto the sofa, the familiarity of the setting erasing the decorum of her adulthood so that a glimpse of her twelve-year-old self could peek through, just for a moment. "And he's not that handsome."

"If you say so. Shall I ring for tea, or something stronger?"

"Something stronger I think."

Theo rang for the butler and ordered their

whiskeys. Once they were settled with their drinks in hand, she spoke again.

"So, was the information you garnered here useful?"

Zoe took a sip of her whiskey. "Yes, it was helpful. You would not believe the day I had yesterday."

She regaled her aunt with the tale of her adventure. Theo listened with intense interest, gasping and oohing at all the right places. It felt good to tell the whole story without risk of judgment or criticism. It wasn't until she had finished the tale that the reality of what she'd done hit her. Zoe took a large swig of her beverage, swallowing quickly.

"That sounds quite exciting. You must really trust this man...Mr. Huxley, was it?"

Zoe thought about that and realized it was true. Down to her bones, she trusted Huxley—Quinton.

"I guess I do, Aunt Theo. He is frustrating and overbearing and difficult, but I do. I trust him."

Theo was quiet for a moment and then spoke gently. "You know he isn't suitable, do you not?"

Zoe said nothing, but Theo must've seen the change in her eyes. She knew when to shift a subject. "Well what brings you by today? Did you just want to tell me about your adventure?"

"Yes, I guess so. I don't know. I'm unsettled. At sixes and sevens."

"Well you're always welcome here, my dear, you know that."

Zoe smiled, putting her thoughts aside. She knew that. Even as a child, isolated and lonely, she'd always felt welcome in this library. Theo always seemed to love having her about, perhaps because she'd never had children of her own.

"I know." Zoe noticed the large book on the table next to her aunt. "Have I interrupted your reading?"

"Oh no, it's nothing terribly interesting." She held up the massive book, *Debrett's Peerage & Baronetage*. "I'm just doing some research on some of the families arriving for the season."

"Do you need to do research? I thought you knew everything." Zoe reached for the decanter and poured another draught. "At least when it came to the peers."

Theo swatted at her. "Don't be smart. I do

pride myself on keeping up to date on the noble families, but there a few families this year that haven't associated with society in quite a while. I'm just brushing up."

"Really? Like whom?"

"The Coleville's for one. The future Earl has kept a low profile, but he's come to introduce his eldest daughter this season. His wife has asked me to help, so I was just doing my due diligence."

"Ah. Well let me know if I can help."

"I would if I thought you meant it." Theo chuckled. "And then there is Lord Driscoll, the Marquess of Kildare."

"Driscoll? I think I met him the other day, at Hyde Park. But I haven't heard the name before."

"No, I'm not surprised. Theirs is a peerage that goes all the way back to the Conqueror himself. A Norman invader settling in the new land who claimed the daughter of a Gaelic king as his bride, and got a title for his trouble. The Driscoll's are an ancient breed, older than most of the British peerages. But they keep to themselves. A Driscoll hasn't crossed the threshold into England in a hundred years."

Zoe cleared her throat. "Huh. Well that's very eccentric of them."

"Indeed. Marquess Driscoll will cause quite a stir among the *ton*, not least of all because he's also brought his son—his single son, heir to his title. Every noble mother will be pushing her daughter into his path." Theo cocked her head. "Maybe you should take a look while you have the chance."

"I don't think so, but thank you for thinking of me, Aunt Theo."

"Why not? I thought you liked eccentrics. Is it because you have your eye on someone else? Maybe a certain not-that-handsome friend by the name of Huxley."

Zoe rolled her eyes. "Now you sound like my mother."

"Your mother wants the best for you."

"So she says." Zoe paused, then spoke. "But what if I did find him handsome, or charming, or interesting? Would that be so terrible? I am already an outcast in society, so the fall wouldn't be too far for me. You certainly get away with all sorts of eccentricities."

"My status and age give me a freedom that single girls your age don't have. It isn't fair, but that is how the world works." Her aunt regarded her thoughtfully. "I do not hold your youth and inexperience against you. But marrying a thief-taker wouldn't just be eccentric or slightly scandalous—it would shatter your reputation, but your families by extension. Everything your mother has worked to build would crumble overnight. Even Phoebes prospects in the distant future would be tainted."

A flush crept up Zoe's neck. "He isn't a thief-taker."

She knew she sounded like a pouting child. Zoe sat up straighter composing herself. When she spoke again, the sulk was gone.

"He isn't a thief taker. And things are changing. Look at the Bluestocking meetings held here, where women are welcome to give serious opinions on politics and science, even disagreeing with the men present. A few years ago that would've been considered scandalous."

Zoe considered her next words, sorting out her thoughts as she went. "I make no claim on Quinton, and as far as I know he thinks of me notably as an absolute nuisance. But I do make claims on my life. He and I are, friends, of a sort, and I am not willing to let that pass by, at least not yet." Zoe stood with her drink; she was prone to pace. "You told me at the beginning of this journey that if I felt strongly enough about something, I should do something about it. That I needed to be true to myself. I won't make any decisions that will rain down fire and ruin for the entire Dovefield brood. But these people are now in my life, and I won't burn any bridges either. They mean something to me, Quinton included."

When she stopped speaking, her back was to Theo, and when she turned to face her, her blue eyes were defiant and her mind made up. Her aunt regarded her, then patted the seat next to her on the divan. Zoe took the invitation.

When she was settled, Theo spoke. "It is so odd to me that when you have that look in your eye, when nothing will sway you, you remind me so much of Hugh. He had that same look when he announced his engagement to your mother. Baldwin and Father tried to talk him out of it, but it was obvious to me his mind was made up. And it has worked out for him—I know he has no regrets. But do not think it came without a price. Many an invitation does not find its way to Hugh's door because of his decision—not just socially, but regarding politics and business as well. Hugh rose above this. He found a different way, and it worked out well."

Theo leaned back and took a thoughtful sip. "Perhaps we can reach our own agreement. I don't know your new friends well, and that we can remedy. I can invite them all here with the thought of getting to know them better, and you can remember your words to bring no scandal on Hugh and Simone. Speak to me before you make any decisions regarding your future. I will support you, and give advice hard earned from my experience, both good and bad, but only if you tell me first. In the meantime, you can keep your eyes open to, um, other possibilities."

Zoe ignored the latter phrase and focused on the offer. "I think my current friends might raise a few eyebrows in this house."

Theo scoffed. "You have no idea what parties these walls have seen, and the characters that have graced these rooms have already raised the necessary eyebrows. Your Uncle Sebastian, for instance. What fun we've had at his parties."

Zoe narrowed her eyes. Sebastian had never married, and certain rumors floated from time to time about the reasons.

"Scandal might find you, Aunt Theo, even with your status."

"Well, I certainly hope so! Let's just say your friends will not be my downfall." Theo laughed and patted her on the hand. "But your stories have enthralled me. I'm a crippled, old lady now, but I am not quite ready for the sidelines." She looked around her beautiful home, filled with priceless paintings and costly furniture. "I've done well for myself. But don't think my husband's money and title didn't help, even after his death. And just because I have chosen a life alone doesn't mean I'm never lonely."

"You are hardly crippled, Aunt Theo, and you have a multitude of interesting friends. "

"And now I can have some young ones again. When this whole fiasco is behind us, I'll make the arrangements."

Chapter Twenty-Two

Quinton woke with a start, sitting up abruptly, the dark tendrils of a nightmare receding to the fuzzy edges of his memory. He pushed the thick blanket off and swung his legs off the bed. The cold wooden floorboards were enough to sober him from the heavy weight of sleep. He shivered as he made his way toward the hearth.

His housekeeper came three times a week to clean and prepare a few meals, but this wasn't one of those days, so he was forced to fend for himself. Some heat was still radiating off the iron fireback and hob grate. Quinton shoveled some coal into the opening, reigniting the simmering fire. He lingered a few moments, enjoying the luxurious heat on his bare toes.

It didn't take him long to clean up with the basin of water and cloth next to his bed. He dressed in a fresh shirt and vest and shaved in the mirror. Zoe had sent word that she and Mary were coming at 11:00 AM and he didn't want to look slovenly.

His office was in the front of the small building; really, just the other side of the room. Quinton entered and tidied the desk, trying to see the space from an outsiders perspective. Then he had urgent personal business to attend to.

It was on his way back from the privy that he saw her—a girl, dressed in the usual threadbare clothes of the street. As he approached, she reached into the depths of her stained skirt and pulled out a note.

"Miss Abigail got a scribble for ya," she said, meeting his eyes. "S'posed ta dabble for a scribble back."

Quinton skimmed the note: *We need to talk. It's important. Come to my flat after tonight's performance.* It was signed with Abigail's customary sweeping A.

Hurriedly, Quinton gave an answer that

he would be there, and gave both his answer and a coin to the girl. He couldn't help but be curious about what Abigail needed. Whatever it was, would have to wait. He watched as the urchin ran off into the increasing traffic before turning back to his more pressing tasks.

∼

Zoe and Mary arrived promptly at Quinton's office at 11, unfashionably early for the gentry, but fine with Zoe. She had never gotten past being an early riser. As they entered, Quinton was behind his desk, with the cat curled up in his lap. Oscar opened a lazy eye to greet the ladies, but otherwise didn't move, her tail covering her paws. Quinton looked up.

"Zoe. Mary." He used Zoe's given name without hesitation this time. "I wasn't sure you would come after last night. I thought you might take a day to recover. Unpleasant business."

Zoe sat quickly in one of the chairs facing the desk, and Mary helped herself to the other. "We wanted news of the dog."

Her tone was surprisingly cheerful. She

gets happier as the plot gets messier, thought Quinton. What a mad girl. He absentmindedly stroked Oscar's fur.

"What's his name again?" Zoe pointed to the cat.

"Oscar." Mary and Quinton spoke as one. Quinton continued. "But he's a she."

Zoe raised her eyebrows. "Her name is Oscar?"

"My friend dropped her off as a wee mite. Orange cats are generally male, so I named it Oscar. The kittens she had proved otherwise." Oscar seemed to sense the conversation had turned to her and stretched. She made her way to the desk, sat regally and looked Zoe over with an intelligent gaze that Zoe returned.

"Is she pregnant now?" Zoe gestured vaguely to Oscar's less than svelte middle.

"No, she's not." The words were clipped—he took her question somewhat personally. Oscar was not starving anymore, but fat? He scoffed inwardly—hardly. "In fact, she only had the one litter. Rory made sure of that."

"He took out her lady bits?" Mary was quick to ask.

"Well, I am not..." Quinton's color rose as he shifted in his chair.

"Unsexed her, then," Mary offered helpfully.

"No, hardly that..." Quinton refused to meet either lady's gaze, clearing his throat.

"Desexed her then. If she had her girl bits she would still..."

"Stop." Quinton's voice was louder than he intended, but Mary was clearly ready to continue. It was obvious from the laughter she was struggling to contain that she was enjoying his discomfort a little too much.

"I don't actually know exactly what he did," he said before he could be embarrassed further. "Rory dropped by after the kittens were weaned and said he could help. The babies went to some friends in need of mousers. But he said he could make sure I didn't need to worry about my Oscar having any more litters. Rory grew up on a farm in Scotland and he knows a lot about the inner workings animals as well as people. And he doesn't hold with drowning unwanted offspring, which I can respect."

He paused to stroke the cat, finally looking at the girls. "He brought her back two days later, and she slept for two more days. Rory came by after a week or two and removed stitches. After that she seemed perfectly normal, but there have been no more kittens."

Quinton finally stopped talking, wondering why he felt compelled to explain. "Regardless, Rory took the dog. He said the injuries aren't so bad. Once you decide what you're going to do with such a creature, you should probably make some kind of arrangements to pick it up."

Mary chuckled, giving Zoe an amused glance. "I am guessing the dog won't be having kittens anymore either."

Zoe laughed out loud—even Quinton allowed a smile.

"I suppose not." Zoe leaned back in her chair, a thoughtful expression on her face. "I think in this case, asking forgiveness will be better than asking permission. I'll go pick up my new dog and once I get a feel for his personality, then I'll know better where his place in the household will be."

"Some free advice, caring for a pet is a lot of work." Quinton gestured to Oscar. "I don't have staff per se, so I spend a good portion of evenings combing her fur for fleas. There's also occasional bathing, plus providing food and water. With cats, the...waste is less of a problem. With a dog though, if he's living in the house, he'll need to be taken out several times a day."

"Oh. I guess you're right, I just hadn't thought about all that yet. I suppose I'll have to hire someone for some of the daily care."

Quinton nonchalantly moved a pencil from one side of his desk to the other. "Well, if you are looking to hire someone, I may have a candidate in mind. Depending on the temperament of the animal."

Zoe shrugged. "I trust your judgment; If you have a candidate, send them my way. We can work out the details later."

It was a high compliment, and Quinton took it as such. Before she could continue, the door opened to reveal an older laborer holding his hat in his hands. Somewhere north of fifty, his hands were rough, and he wore an apologetic expression.

"Beggin' your pardon, Mr. Huxley. I didn't know you was with anyone."

"Mr. Loughty. Please, come in for a moment—I'm nearly finished here anyway. I have been working on your dilemma, but I haven't quite found a solution within the scope of the law. I apologize for the delay—I do have some alternative options to consider..."

"I have some legal experience," Zoe interjected. "What is the question?"

The man glanced at Quinton questioningly. He hesitated, thinking of what John had said. If the girl really had grown up at the knee of one of the great barristers of his generation, perhaps she could help.

"I got a neighbor who has been trying to buy me out for a bit now. I don't have much, but I live in the home my daddy built, and I own it proper. When my daddy passed, it came to me." The man stood straighter with the pride of ownership, as well he should. In his class, he was in the minority. "He made me an offer, as he gots much more than me, but I want to live where I live. It's my home. That's when the threats started. He is right determined to get my place and he thinks maybe he can scare me out. So I was just hoping Mr. Huxley could find a way to make him stop, within the law and all."

Mr. Loughty took a deep breath and

looked down, continuing to wring the hat in his hands.

"Has he threatened bodily harm or have the threats taken a written form?" Zoe asked.

"He has threatened all kinds of harm and sent me two letters. They aren't too pleasant for the ears of a lady."

"Nonsense. Threatening behavior falls under 'Breaking the Peace' in the eyes of the law. The presence of the letters is viable proof of this conduct. It's a misdemeanor, so it would be tried in the Sessions of the Peace, not Old Bailey, but perhaps if Mr. Huxley makes it plain there is legal action to be taken, your neighbor will restrain himself." She tucked a strand of hair behind her ear. "And if that doesn't work, I would consider taking Mr. Huxley up on his alternative options."

The room was still as the other three souls took stock of her speech.

Zoe was unperturbed. "I would be happy to word letters detailing his offense, as well as what the consequences of his actions could be if he chooses to continue his behavior. If Mr. Huxley is agreeable."

Quinton cleared his throat, leaning forward on his desk. "If that is agreeable with you, Mr. Loughty, we can have them delivered by post tomorrow. You can let me know if further action is needed."

Mr. Loughty smiled gratefully, and after thanking them all several times, he left.

"You are full of surprises...Zoe." Quinton saw the temperamental girl through fresh eyes.

She shrugged. "My father is a barrister, Mr. Huxley. I have learned our family business. If you will pass me ink and quill, I can write out those letters now, and then we can discuss your candidates."

Chapter Twenty-Three

The evening air was brisk enough to make Quinton shiver, even while wearing his overcoat. He had a more formal greatcoat, but he usually wore this simple one, hanging just above his knees, and heavy enough to keep out the wind.

He grimaced as he glanced back at the urchins following him. Gwen told him that the necklace had attracted too much unwanted attention, and finally Ezra had made her sell it. Quinton suspected that's where the sturdy boots they both wore came from. But they still lacked coats. The pantaloons Gwen wore under her dirty muslin shift offered little protection from the autumn elements. Ezra wore breeches, somehow both too wide and too short, held up by suspenders over a dirty and hole ridden shirt.

Quinton refocused his attention on the path ahead. He hoped this idea of having the children take care of Zoe's new dog would work out. The urchins had occupied a significant space in his thoughts since he met them. He'd even sought Ezra out a time or two to run written messages for him. Although London was overflowing with waifs, something about these two gave him pause. There was something about them...

Maybe it was Ezra's height, or the sharp glint of intelligence in Gwen's eyes. More than anything, he supposed he admired their loyalty to each other. Girls younger than Gwen made money at the workhouses, or in worse ways. But he saw how Ezra went without so she could eat, protecting her from the dangers lurking on the streets. On the other side, anyone could see how Gwen spoke and listened for them both, making sure his deafness didn't make him vulnerable.

The girl must've been starved for conversation as she talked nonstop as they walked. Quinton reflected it must be hard for a chatty child like Gwen to spend most of her time with a brother who could not speak—although he supposed they spoke in their own way.

Distantly, he heard Gwen telling him about a close call she had with a runaway carriage. Street children were routinely crushed beneath wagons and carriages, and usually the owner did not even bother to stop. After all, they were just urchins, invisible and dispensable. Crush one, and there were a hundred to take their place.

Quinton only half listened as Gwen described the incident. She said a man had pulled her to safety just as the carriage passed. He spoke to her and had even given her a coin. She had a quick eye, that girl, and described him in detail, including his Hussein boots, Wellington hat, foreign accent, and caped overcoat. Quinton was grateful to the gentleman.

As Gwen went into a similarly detailed description of the horses, Quinton returned to his own thoughts. It was a morbid reality, but he reckoned that near miss was a blessing in its own way. It was likely the only reason Ezra had agreed to go to the Dovefield's to see about the job. He realized he couldn't keep Gwen safe forever.

They arrived at the stately home, and Quinton glanced at Ezra. He could tell from the crossed arms and glowering frown the boy was struggling with the idea of this change. The devil, you know, thought Quinton. Everyone loves progress, but everyone hates change.

"I have an appointment so I can't wait with you but Lady Demas is an excellent lady and will take care of both of you, should you wish it. You'll have a roof over your heads, as well as a bed and three meals a day."

Ezra watched his lips move closely. He was still for a moment, processing the words, then gestured to his sister and nodded, before pointing at himself and shaking his head.

"No!" Gwen instantly grasped his meaning. "Either both of us go or none of us go!"

Quinton could hear the fear in her voice. Ezra shook his head, and tears came to Gwen's eyes as she spoke in reply.

"We ain't never been apart Ezra. I won't go without you."

Ezra continued to gesture. Finally he reached down, taking Gwen's chin in his hand

and locking eyes with her. He made one last movement with his hand. Quinton couldn't yet understand the boy's way of communicating, but even he grasped the meaning.

Gwen nodded reluctantly. "I love you, too, Ezra. I'll make money for us both. Just you come see me right often."

Quinton understood. Having lived on the streets for a decent chunk of his childhood, he knew how hard it was to trust. Life was difficult for a homeless orphan, but while you were alone, you were master of your own fate. Giving up that freedom and control was harder for some than others.

"He'll wait with me for the lady, but he ain't ready to give up the streets."

"I understand." Quinton clasped her shoulder. "I'll keep an eye on him."

"You don't owe us nothin' Mr. Quinton, and you already helped us plenty, but I'd be grateful. I can't be 'is ears if I am living in a house."

"He'll be fine, Gwen. Right now, just focus on winning over Lady Demas."

Gwen smiled. The sparkle was back, ready for her new adventure.

"Done."

Chapter Twenty-Four

Prying the dog out of Rory's hands had been more of an ordeal than Zoe expected. Not that he'd grown attached or anything—it was that he never stopped talking. Details on the care of the beast, on keeping its broken leg immobile, and the value of Shakespeare for interpreting romantic signals. Zoe wasn't sure what the last thing had to do with taking care of a dog, but she assumed there was some connection in Rory's mind. He was a strange man, that one.

The dog lay on the other side of the hackney. Its bulk took up the entire seat, tongue lolling out as he panted. He seemed remarkably cheerful considering his recent brush with death.

Mary gave her a side eye. "Are you quite sure about this?"

"Well I'm not sure what else to do. I started this whole thing. I think at this point I have some level of responsibility in his fate."

"Perhaps. But we could find some other arrangements for him. Maybe a farm or something..."

Zoe contemplated this while the dog's dark eyes contemplated her. She'd never had a pet before. Much of her early childhood was spent alone. It wasn't that it was unhappy; she had very fond memories of playing with her father on their estate, and stealing pastries from the kitchen, and painting with her mother. But she also remembered sitting in her room, playing with dolls by herself, or wandering the halls just waiting for something to happen. Simone always said their family was so perfect that they'd never wanted another addition. But it had been lonely.

Then when they came to England, she was still alone. Even when Simone married Hugh and added to their family with two new children, Zoe was on her own much of the time. Her new siblings were babies, and her mother and stepfather had new obligations.

She didn't know if a pet would've made a difference. But the idea of having a creature in her life who wanted to be with her, without judgment or reservation, made her feel... something. Zoe liked the idea of not being alone quite so much anymore.

"I don't want him to go to a farm." Zoe reached out and stroked the top of his enormous head. His fur was softer than she expected. He didn't make a sound, but leaned into her touch. She could already hear her mother's objections: he's too big, too ugly, too dangerous. She would say he didn't belong in their world. But Zoe often thought she didn't belong there either.

Mary sighed. "Well I can see you have your mind set on it. I assume you know it's going to go over like a sack of rocks tossed into the Thames."

"Yes. But I think I can minimize the damage. Hopefully Quinton's 'candidates' comes through."

As they pulled up in front of her home, Zoe turned to Mary. "Go fetch James—actually get that new footman too. James isn't as strong as Quinton; he won't be able to lift the dog on his own."

Mary nodded and dashed out of the hackney. Zoe followed behind her, bracing herself for the inevitable storm. That's when she saw them.

The two children looked very forlorn standing in front of the gate. Quinton said he would bring his "candidates" by, but Zoe assumed he would stay with them. He told her they were urchins, and of course she was familiar with the concept of street children. But there was something about the contrast of seeing the two of them, all by themselves, against the backdrop of her grand house that sent a chill up her spine.

"Wait here, please," Zoe told the coachman as she moved toward the children.

The boy was tall, but thin as a rail. He wore a cap pulled down low over his eyes and leaned against the fence with his arms crossed. The girl was petite—even if she wasn't half starved, Zoe could see her bone structure was slight of build. Despite her small stature, she stood straighter than the boy. Both wore threadbare clothes and their faces and hands were smeared with grime.

The girl's bright eyes watched her walk over, sizing her up. Quinton had mentioned the girl—Gwen—was sharp, and Zoe believed it.

"Hello there." Zoe held out a hand, trying not to think about where the other hand had been. "You must be Gwen."

"Lady Demas." The girl gripped her hand firmly and then gestured to the boy. "And this is my brother, Ezra."

"A pleasure." Zoe extended the hand to him as well. He took it more reluctantly than his sister. It took all her self control not wipe the grime off on her frock.

She turned back to Gwen. "Where is Mr. Huxley?"

"He said he had an appointment he couldn't be late for."

"Of course he did," Zoe muttered. "Very well. Do either of you have any experience with animals?"

"Not particularly, ma'am. But we're quick learners and hard workers."

"Uh huh. And your parents?"

"Both dead, ma'am. Cholera."

Ezra grunted and moved his hands, gesturing at Gwen. Quinton said the boy was deaf, but Zoe hadn't been sure what to expect. She'd met no one deaf before.

"My brother can understand you better if you look directly at him when you speak."

"Ah, of course." Zoe cleared her throat. "Well come over here, both of you."

She led them over to the hackney where the dog still lay. "I assume Mr. Huxley explained the situation?"

"Yes." Gwen eyed the beast. "His description didn't do it justice."

Ezra made a movement with his hands that even Zoe didn't need interpreted.

"You're right, he is quite large. I would understand if either of you were put off by that."

The siblings exchanged a glance. Ezra looked very uneasy, but Gwen's expression didn't change. She was a bold girl, Zoe would give her that.

Gwen reached out a hand, and the dog sniffed it. She gestured for Ezra to do the same, but he just shook his head. She sighed, resigned to his decision. For the first time, the boy made eye contact with Zoe. She understood—he wasn't afraid of the dog. He wanted his sister to get the job. He wasn't afraid; he was sad.

"It's alright, Gwen." Zoe turned back to the girl. "What do you think of him? Would you be comfortable taking care of him?"

By this point the dog was scratching at the floor, impatient with its confinement. Gwen stepped up and into the hackney and began stroking its head. The beast leaned into her hand, seeming to enjoy the attention.

"I think so, ma'am."

"It won't be a simple job. He's lived a hard life. And once his wounds heal, you'll need to train him and be able to keep control of him."

"I understand." Gwen looked back at her brother. "Are you sure, Ezra?"

The boy nodded. A pang of sympathy struck Zoe.

"We might be able to find a position for you too. Perhaps in the stables."

He shook his head and gestured to his sister. "He says he's not ready for that. But he wants me to stay here. He wants me to be safe."

"Very well." Zoe nodded. "Gwen, say your goodbyes, and then I'll take you around to the back entrance so you can get cleaned up and a change of clothes." She looked again at Ezra. "You're welcome to visit anytime."

"I don't want to stay without you," said Gwen.

It was the first time Zoe had seen a crack in her composure. Ezra took her hand and pulled her over to the side. They communicated silently, through their own secret language, but Zoe could guess the gist of it.

"What in heavens name is going on!"

That was the sound she'd been bracing for. Her mother was standing outside the gate, mouth open with a hand on her forehead.

"Hello, *mama*."

"Don't 'hello *mama*' me. Mary has rounded up both the footmen in order to carry a dog into our home?! What is going on?" Simone's eyes locked on the urchins. "And what are these children doing here?"

By now, Mary had finally come out with the footmen in question. Zoe addressed them.

"You two"—she still couldn't think of that new footman's name—"take the dog up into my room. Mary, could you please take Gwen around back?"

"Of course, milady."

While the servants followed instructions, Zoe looked at her mother. She could practically see the steam coming out of her ears. Hugh often said Simone never looked more beautiful than when she was angry. Zoe wasn't sure about that, but she certainly made an impression.

"Mother, I understand this must all be very confusing for you right now. Come inside with me and I will explain."

"Zoe Demas, you better explain this right this instant—"

"I will," Zoe interrupted. "But we need to go inside. Honestly, Mother, you're making a scene."

Zoe walked back towards the house, leaving her mother still open-mouthed. She'd won that battle and they both knew it. She also knew that brief comment wouldn't go over well in the following discussion, but Zoe just couldn't resist getting the last jab in.

Chapter Twenty-Five

Quinton had just arrived back at his office when John burst in. He knew his friend well; it only took one glance to know something was terribly wrong.

"Where have you been? I've been trying to reach you all day, Q. I already stopped by twice."

His first thought was of Zoe—with her maddening, stubborn, impossible ways. The way her hair escaped its pins and the way her blue eyes turned dark when a storm was coming. His heart dropped into his stomach and for a moment he could not speak.

John rushed on, too fired up to notice Quinton's stillness. "I have bad news."

His expression was one of such dread and regret, Quinton thought his heart would explode with anticipation. He almost didn't want him to say whatever was next. Once it was spoken, it was real. While it still hung in the silence, whatever terrible thing had happened hadn't happened to him yet. It wasn't logical, but as long as John didn't say it, it wasn't yet real.

"It's Abigail. She's dead."

The words were like a punch to his stomach. He gasped, reaching absently for his chair, falling into it more than sitting down on it. His first feeling was relief that it wasn't Zoe, followed by immediate guilt.

"How...what happened? Are you sure? She sent me a note to meet her tonight..." His voice trailed off into silence.

"I'm sure, Q. I seen her myself." John's voice was so low, it could barely be heard. Or maybe he was speaking at a normal volume, but Quinton couldn't hear over the ringing in his ears.

John stared at him, waiting for a reply, but Quinton couldn't think of anything rational to say. Eventually, John walked around the desk to the drawer that held the whiskey and glasses. He pulled out two glasses, followed by the bottle. It was only after both he and Quinton held a full glass before he spoke again.

"Bow Street's been wound up real tight this past month. The magistrate's playing it close to the chest, but everyone's on edge. He's been telling us to keep an eye out for dead girls. Not one's who died like Lucy, where it looks like an accident, but ones where they were killed real obvious like. So when someone reported a dead girl in a boarding house near Covent Garden, I was real quick to get there. Wasn't what the magistrate was looking for, but I recognized her right away." John took a large swig of whiskey. "I'm right sorry, Q. I know she meant a great deal to you. She was part of your world before you found our world, part of your mama's world, and that ain't somethin' you can replace."

He brought his own glass to his lips automatically, but as the whiskey burned his throat, it revived him back to the land of the living. He sucked in a shuddering breath, the full pain of his loss hitting him for the first time. John was right. Abigail meant—had meant—a great deal to him.

"How did she die?" Quinton spoke softly, his voice barely above a whisper.

"Her head was struck. More than once by the looks of it. I pulled some strings to have her sent to Rory's, after the coroners finished of course. Your resurrectionist does know how to talk to the dead."

Quinton nodded his understanding, leaning back and closing his eyes. Both he and John were no strangers to death, to sadness, to heartbreak. Quinton knew the pain would work through him, eventually finding its way out in its own time. He rose slowly, glass in hand, and headed for the overstuffed chair by the fire, settling in as John followed. He always found the warmth of the fire comforting.

"I knew Abigail practically since she was born, and her me. We grew up together in that theater. It doesn't seem possible she's..."

John's reply was quiet, respecting the tone of the room.

"I know, Q. I know. I remember." He smiled, leaning back in his own chair. "Every now and again you would sneak Charlie and I into the back of that old theater, and Abigail would play with us in those hallways. Always an extra place to hide behind some stage fixin's, or some extra clothes to make up a costume."

Quinton laughed, despite the tears falling down his cheeks. "True. I didn't get over to see her as much as I used to these days. I was just so busy..."

"She loved you, Q. You didn't need to explain yourself to her."

There was nothing to be said to that, so Quinton ignored it. What they'd spoken of the last time he saw her came to mind. "She knew Lucy when she first came to London. Didn't quite say it in so many words, but I could tell they were close—really close. Called in a favor to get Lucy the job with the Dovefield's."

"She was a kind person."

"She was—sometimes to a fault." The reality of her death weighed on Quinton's chest. "I was only stopping off to change before I went to see her. If I hadn't delayed..."

John shook his head. "Don't do that, Q. What if, could have, should have—you and I both know there's no good to be found down that road. It wouldn't have made a difference anyway. She died earlier in the day, probably right after she sent you that note."

It helped to know that a few minutes' difference wouldn't have mattered, but the guilt still gnawed at his insides. He took another swig of whiskey. With each sip, his senses came back to him.

Quinton sat up straighter, his first rational thought forming since hearing the news. "This cannot be a coincidence, her death on the heels of Lucy's death. Abigail was going to tell me something, and that something must have gotten her killed."

He stood up swiftly, looking John in the eye. "Thank you for coming here to tell me about Abigail yourself. I will have time to grieve later, but right now there's no time. Right now I need to get to Rory's."

Chapter Twenty-Six

Quinton wondered, not for the first time, if Rory's neighbors knew what he did for a living. The delivery of the legal bodies must be no secret, though his more clandestine activities might be less known. Zoe was right about one thing. Rory was a man of contradictions.

He knocked firmly on the solid front door, but the house was quiet. He knew why. Reluctantly he turned to the cobbled path that ran from the door through the small garden to the outbuilding. When he drew closer, he could hear a cheerful tune being whistled. Rory was really never happier than when he had a new body to decipher. He knew he meant nothing by it, but this time it soured his stomach.

"Is that an Irish drinking song or a Scottish funeral dirge? I can never tell the difference." Quinton tried to act normal as he opened the door, just joking with his old friend, but then he saw the body.

It was indeed Abigail, but her face was hardly recognizable beneath all the blood. She was so still...he took a deep breath to steady himself.

"Easy, lad. I know she was a friend of yours. We don't need to have a conversation here." Rory grasped Quinton by the shoulder, attempting to guide him outside.

Quinton remained immovable, staring at Abigail's still body. "How did she die?"

His voice was flat even to his own ears, but he knew it was no emotion, or far too much.

Rory slid his body between the corpse and Quinton, blocking his gaze. "I'll tell you over some strong coffee up at the house."

His grip tightened, and finally Quinton nodded, following him back up the cobbled path, this time into the house. Rory didn't speak until after he'd poured them both a cup of the promised brew.

"So this lass and your lady's lass have a few things in common. I've not had a chance to do a full exam, but the way they died isn't dissimilar."

"She's not my lady," Quinton muttered automatically, but Rory ignored him.

"They both died from repeated blows to the back of the head. I can't say for certain it's the same hand that did it, but I can say the manner is consistent. I know the maid is a case of yours, and I know this lass is a friend of yours, so I canna help but believe this death has to do with that one."

"I agree. Abigail had more to tell me. I was supposed to meet with her tonight."

"What a shame." Rory shook his head. "There are some interesting contrasts that I believe shed some light on the motives of the killer, if indeed it was the same."

Quinton leaned forward. "Such as?"

"The maid died quickly. She didn't have any abrasions on her hands or arms—I don't think she ever saw it coming. Her death was calculated. But the actress was different. She saw it coming and she fought like 'ell. I think her death came from a place of passion more than calculation. I think this man lost his temper and killed 'er in a fit of rage."

Quinton's own rage boiled within him. "So he meant to kill Lucy, but Abigail was a spur of the moment thing?"

"It's a working theory. But I'd be careful with this one, lad. He's a violent one. I don't think he'll hesitate to do the same to anyone else that stands in his way."

"He's nothing but a coward, Rory. He'll react differently when he's faced with a grown man such as myself."

"Don't be too cocky, Quinton. Men who are willing to kill usually find a way."

"Maybe." There was no point in arguing about it. "How do you know Abigail defended herself?"

"Her knuckles. They're scraped raw. And there's blood on the front of her dress, quite a lot, near the hem. I canna see where her head wound in the back would stain the front of her dress where I found these heavy drops of blood. And then there's her right hand. She has a cut on it—a deep one. Usually I see these particular cuts when the person themselves is wielding a knife, and they stab hard enough the blade backs up from the outward blow and cuts the wielder. Especially if they're using a small knife with little hilt to stop it. Was she a lass who carried a knife?"

Quinton immediately pictured the knife in his mind. A petite blade with an ivory handle, sharper than its feminine look, appeared. He'd given it to Abigail as a present many years ago; a weapon for when she had to protect herself against the fanatical men whose adoration turned to stalking.

"She carried a knife."

"Well, lad, she used it. I'd bet good money someone out there carries a wound to match. Find the wound, and I believe you will find your murderer."

Chapter Twenty-Seven

The conversation went the way Zoe expected. Her mother and she ranted and raved at each other in French while Hugh sat quietly, waiting for the storm to blow over.

Once the fire had mostly burned itself out, he suggested they take a few days to consider their options. A compromise would have to be reached, but not today. Zoe knew it annoyed her mother just as much as her when Hugh started talking in his lawyer voice, calm and placating.

Simone agreed to let the matter lay for now, on one condition—Hugh's younger brother Sebastian was in town and Aunt Theo was celebrating with a dinner party. Of course, they were invited. The condition was that Zoe would attend.

She normally did her best to avoid such occasions; at least at a ball there was the opportunity to lose oneself in the crowd. Dinner parties were intimate occasions where meaningless small talk was not just expected, but required. There was no way to blend into the wallpaper when you were required to converse with the person next to you.

Despite her reservations, Zoe agreed to attend. She had spent much of her parents good grace in the past few days, and this seemed a petty thing to make an issue of in the larger scheme of things.

So while the housekeeper settled Gwen and the brute into the house, Mary prepared her for the trial ahead. It involved bathing and hair styling, which she had to admit Mary was very good at. She'd never had a maid before who could tame her wild curls into a semblance of order, while still keeping some of her natural look. Looking in the mirror, it made her feel…more comfortable in her own skin. Less like a foreigner.

They decided on half-dress for the occasion, with a flattering but simple light green gown and modest embellishments tucked into her hair. It was important to look presentable, but one didn't want to do full-dress as if for a ball and then risk being the most ostentatious one there.

Simone eyed her like a general inspecting his troops when she came down the stairs, but it seemed Zoe did indeed pass muster. Not that she would admit it to her mother, but when she looked at the full effect in her mirror before coming down, even she was pleased with the result.

Only the three adults—Hugh, Simone, and Zoe—were invited. Children weren't expected to be present at social events until they were in their late teens and old enough to be considered adult company. Of course, Walter and Phoebe still pouted at the exclusion, but Zoe assured them they were the lucky ones before kissing them on the cheek and sending them off with the governess.

By the time they arrived at Theo's home, it was already 9:00 pm. If her party was a success, it would last into the early hours of the morning, and Theo's parties were always a success. Zoe braced herself for the hours of tedium to come.

They were ushered into the sitting room and announced by Benson. Zoe quickly snatched a glass of white wine off a tray.

Theo greeted them warmly. "Ah, there you are. I think you know the Coleville's, but there's a few unfamiliar faces I'll introduce you to."

Zoe was only vaguely familiar with the Coleville's, but greeted them as if they were old friends. She hadn't met their daughter Amelia before, as this was her first season. The girl was a pretty enough thing, though so pale one could see the blue veins under the skin of her temples and wrists. Zoe wondered if she suffered from migraines.

Theo pivoted as Benson entered to announce another group of arriving guests, this time beating him to the punch. "And this is Marquess Patrick Driscoll and his son, Earl Brian Driscoll."

Zoe nearly choked on her wine. "Ahem, yes, we've, uh, met."

She glared at her aunt as she recalled their conversation about other possibilities. Theo met her eyes with absolute innocence.

"Ah yes, I do remember you." Lord Driscoll laughed. "I supposed it's inevitable that we would run into each other again. It is after all the London season."

Having just arrived, the father son duo both still wore their top hats and greatcoats. Zoe wondered how they got past Benson with their outerwear intact.

Heat burned Zoe's cheeks. Theo hadn't been very subtle. He would assume she was trying to catch his son's eye, and that this entire dinner party had been orchestrated so he could meet two of the season's eligible ladies. It was humiliating.

Lord Driscoll seemed oblivious to her discomfort. "This is my son, Brian."

Benson appeared as if out of thin air at the men's sides to take their hat and coats, and the elder Driscoll turned to speak with him as he handed over his outerwear. Zoe's attention rested on the younger Driscoll.

The young man bore a striking resemblance to his father, twenty years younger of course. He had the same green eyes and red hair beneath his hat, but was blessed with a charming lopsided smile.

"A pleasure to make your acquaintance," he said, his Irish accent distinct, but not as pronounced as his father. He started to hold out his right hand, but then switched to his left with a wince.

"The pleasure is mine, Lord Driscoll," she said, taking his hand. The reply was automatic—just a part of the script.

"Ah, if it isn't my favorite niece!"

Zoe turned to see her favorite uncle, the guest of honor. It was a welcome interruption to the awkward meeting of Brian Driscoll.

"It's so good to see you, Sebastian! Why didn't you tell me you were in town?"

Sebastian Dovefield was the youngest of the original Dovefield brood. Theo claimed in his youth that half the eligible young ladies had been after him, and Zoe could imagine it. He'd been devastatingly handsome, not to mention charming and kind, as well as a true gentleman. It didn't seem to matter that he had no inheritance. But to the heartbreak of many a damsel, he never took a wife.

Now he was in his early forties, and though there were a few subtle signs of aging, like the graying hairs on his temple and the fine lines in the corner of his eyes, he was still a very handsome man. He had lost none of his charm, either. For his adult life, he was given a small allowance, first from his father and then from Baldwin, but he lived well beyond his means, mainly through the hospitality of others. Sebastian had friends in Barcelona, Milan, India, and even the colonies—America, it was called now. They paid for his travel and bestowed extravagant gifts, and he would stay there for months at a time. His "friends" raised eyebrows in certain circles, but no one actually spoke the rumors out loud. It was the scandal that most of society turned a blind eye to.

"I got in late last night," said Sebastian. "I've hardly had time to breathe before this party my dear sister concocted."

"Very well, I forgive you. How was New York? Exhilarating and exotic?"

"Well that's one way to describe it." Sebastian took a sip of wine, a mischievous glint in his eye. "You'll have to come with me next time I go."

Zoe's eyes lit up. "I would love to go to New York! Are you sure your friends wouldn't mind?"

"Of course not. In a lot of ways, it's just like here—big houses and country estates with too many bedrooms. There would be plenty of room for you, and I think you're old enough to do some traveling at this point."

"Oh, thank you so much, Uncle!"

"I'll have to discuss it with your parents of course, and I did just get back, so my next trip won't be for some time." Sebastian kissed her on the cheek. "So don't get ahead of yourself, Love."

His attention was taken then by Hugh, signaling the end of their conversation. Zoe knew the two of them hadn't always had an uncomplicated relationship. It was hard enough to bond when the age gap was over a decade, but their childhood had been made more complicated by the death of their mother and the quick remarriage of their father. He'd sent the fifteen-year-old to live with his older sister, but the baby Sebastian had stayed at home as a part of the new family unit. Resentment came as second nature to teenagers, whether or not it was deserved. The men didn't speak of it, but Theo had explained the situation. Fortunately, as adults, they found some common ground.

Zoe sipped her wine and surveyed the rest of the room. She wasn't surprised to see William Garrow was also among the attendees, as he was a regular in their social circle. He was making conversation with the last of the party goers, Lady Charlotte Fairfax, a woman in her seventies. Her husband had died years ago, but occasionally her son accompanied her when his navy ship was in port. Tonight she was alone.

She couldn't be described as a particularity attractive woman, although there was nothing misshapen about her features. She was just...plain. It might not have mattered if she had a personality that could be described as something other than sour. She was often critical and rarely interesting, so Zoe had little time for her, but Theo felt a social obligation to include her. Though she had only met him occasionally, Zoe found it interesting that her son was quite the opposite. He was charming and amusing and, for a man around her stepfather's age, not entirely unattractive.

It wasn't long before the dinner party was ushered into the dining room. Theo had balanced the numbers well, so there was an even number of men and women for conversation. As Zoe had suspected, she was seated next to Brian.

"So how are you finding London, Lord

Driscoll?" Zoe asked, trying to hide her mortification with the small talk she disdained.

"I've found it very entertaining. It's a dynamic city."

"Is it your first time visiting?" asked Zoe, already knowing the answer.

"Yes. The Driscolls prefer to stay on our side of the sea." He gave her that lopsided smile. "We come from a long line of isolationists."

Zoe returned the smile. "Well if that's the case, what's brought you here for this season?"

Brian's eyes turned toward the older Driscoll. "My father is less traditional than our ancestors. He wants me to have access to the opportunities the London season affords."

"Ah, I see. And the rest of your family didn't accompany you?"

His smile faded and a darker emotion flashed in his eyes. "My mother died when I was a child. It's just me and my father now."

"Oh." Zoe blushed. "I'm sorry. I apologize for bringing up such a painful loss."

"There was no way for you to know. It's not the sort of thing that comes up in casual conversation."

"No, I suppose not. But I do understand,

to a degree. My father also passed when I was very young."

Brian's smile returned, although not as bright. "Then you know what it's like. I'm afraid the loss created a rift between my father and me that I didn't believe would ever be healed. But when I returned from university, the time apart seemed to have done us well. For the first time in a long time, I think we're on the same page, which is a refreshing feeling."

"I'm pleased for you, genuinely." Zoe stirred her soup with no intention of eating it. "I do understand the rift that can come with such a loss. I don't think my mother and I found common ground until my younger brother and sister were born. Did your father ever remarry, or do you have any siblings?"

"Do I have any siblings? No. I'm afraid I'm an only child, so all my father's hopes and ambitions must rest with me." Brian's eyes shifted away, and he cleared his throat. "But let's turn our conversation to less depressing topics."

"Of course. Although I fear my mind is filled with only depressing topics these days."

His face softened. "Well I would gladly

discuss someone else's troubles rather than my own. What sad things are on your mind?"

"Oh, nothing that is an appropriate conversation for the dinner table."

"Well in case you haven't noticed, I hardly adhere to the standards of what British upper society would consider appropriate." His lopsided grin was back, but this time it was softer—kinder. "What's troubling you?"

Zoe wasn't sure why she'd found him so off-putting at first. Brian Driscoll seemed like a genuinely nice young man. Certainly better than the usual stuffy heirs and lords she was forced to make casual conversation with.

"If you really want to know...my lady's maid died recently." Zoe hesitated; she didn't know if she should go into too much detail on the investigation she'd launched in the wake of her death. It was a lot to explain, even for someone as unorthodox as Brian Driscoll. "The loss has taken a toll on me these past few days."

"That's dreadful. Was she ill?"

"No. It was a sudden loss."

"Ah. I'm sorry to hear that." Brian's eyes were still soft. "That must've been a terrible shock for you. Were you close with the maid?"

Zoe glanced away. "Not particularly. I think that's part of what's made it so hard. I've lost this person who knew me, intimately, and yet now that I look back, I realize I didn't really know them at all."

"Well that's often the way it is with servants." Brian shrugged. "They know us better than we know them. Did she ever speak of details of her past? About her family or things of that nature?"

"No. She was very private." There was no point in going into all that she'd learned about Lucy since her death. It was much too involved of a conversation to have over dinner. "And I never asked when I had the chance."

"Ah. Perhaps it is for the best. The shock must've been great, but it will be easier for you to move on since you weren't close companions."

"Yes." Zoe turned her attention back to the soup. "Perhaps you are right."

The rest of the dinner passed quicker than usual, and before she knew it, it was time for the ladies to go through. As Zoe stood to follow them out, she took one last look around the table.

She hadn't been paying much attention to

the other guests; Brian had captured her attention. But when her eyes came to rest on his father, for the first time seeing him directly without his outerwear, her blood ran cold.

Patrick Driscoll sat there, laughing at something Sebastian was saying. Zoe was sure it was funny, but a ringing in her ears prevented her from hearing it. She watched him run his fingers through his thick, red hair—red hair marred by a single, white streak that started at his forehead.

Chapter Twenty-Eight

Hugh entered Simone's parlor as quietly as possible, observing her as she sat curled in a chair with a French book in her lap. She still took his breath away, even after all these years. She was a force, that was certain, but he knew her softer side.

He and Simone shared an hour together most evenings. He preferred whiskey, as did Zoe, but Simone enjoyed port, so he always took a glass with her. Quaid always left a bottle out and made sure the staff stayed out of their way. It was their time to talk and connect. Tonight, after returning from Theo's, was no exception.

The family had left the dinner party early

on this occasion. Zoe went deathly pale and barely spoke after dinner. Hugh suspected her extracurricular activities were catching up with her. Exhaustion took a toll, no matter how noble the cause. So Hugh had made their excuses, and they'd departed well before midnight.

"Good book?" Hugh murmured a greeting, as he leaned down to kiss her neck.

His beautiful wife smiled up at him. "It is quite engaging. Not that I have had much time to read it tonight."

Simone was at her most relaxed during this hour with Hugh. Theirs was an equal partnership—a complete meeting of minds and souls, where neither felt the need for pretense or disguise. He could see the stress drain from her body as he handed her a glass of the port, before settling next to her on the settee. She leaned against him and sighed with satisfaction.

Hugh was the first to speak. "So what are we going to do about the dog?"

Simone's face broke into a slight smile. "The brute is more like it. What was she thinking, bringing an animal like that into our home?"

"I can agree the brute is a surprise." Hugh laughed, stretching out his legs and putting his feet up on the matching footstool. "But I have seen a change in Zoe that has also been a surprise—a welcome one. Have you noticed how she no longer complains of boredom? How she arises each day, excited, with a purpose to her step? She's almost...happy, for the first time in a long time. I think perhaps whatever force she's found in her life is for her good."

Simone sipped her port, her face thoughtful. "She has changed to be sure, and she does seem to have a purpose. But at what cost? She's gone until all hours of the day and night, and you and I both know she isn't sticking to the respectable parts of the city. Now she's come home with a fighting dog. How do you suppose she came upon the creature? It wasn't by happenstance in Hyde Park."

"She is finding herself, my dear. Finding her way." Hugh wrapped his arm tighter around her. "We both wish Zoe would find her way more conventionally, but it may be time we faced reality. It's Zoe. She has never been conventional."

"True," Simone said with a sigh.

Hugh chuckled. "Garrow told her yesterday she would have made an excellent woman barrister, if there was such a thing. And he is right."

"I wish he wouldn't encourage her. It just makes it harder for her to accept reality."

They lapsed into silence. It was an old discussion, one they wouldn't agree on soon. Hugh wanted Zoe to reach for the stars. Simone wanted her to accept her place on the ground and make the best of it.

Finally she changed the subject to something more amusing. "Last night as she and Mary were going up the stairs past my room, I heard the words 'Button it up. I am in no mood for your moods. I want a whiskey and my bed.'"

"Zoe can be abrupt at times."

"The maid said that to Zoe. And Zoe laughed."

Hugh scoffed, then laughed out loud. "Perhaps we should increase our whiskey order." He thought for a moment. "We have never been particularly conventional in how we treat our staff, but that girl has found a unique place here. It's good for Zoe to have a companion who challenges her. She's been lonely for too long."

"I agree. But the idea of a companion isn't a bad one. Perhaps that role would be more suited to her temperament. She is a bit forward for a maid."

"We should discuss it with Zoe. But regardless of her title, I believe Mary can handle herself. If Zoe insists on roaming all over London, it's good she has someone like that on her side."

Simone nodded in agreement. "True. Although I think the most impressive thing about her is how she can handle curls. It's never looked so good."

Hugh laughed. "You would think that."

"It's true!" She swatted at him. "You wouldn't appreciate how valuable a skill that is."

"You're right about that." Hugh chuckled to himself. "But we are getting a bit off topic. We were discussing the dog."

"Ah, yes. The dog. I'd almost forgotten about the brute," Simone said with a sigh.

Hugh shrugged. "Many people have dogs for pets."

Simone interrupted. "The Hadlestons have a Pomeranian! Brutes are less common."

"True. But the Hadlestons do not have a grown daughter who prowls the city of London in the twilight hours. I think you and I can agree that we cannot control Zoe. Short of locking her in her room, it seems likely she will continue to follow her heart on this quest. And what better dog for her than a brute who can accompany her and Mary on these travels? I for one will sleep better knowing anyone Zoe meets, wherever she goes, will have to go through both Mary and the brute. Perhaps it is worth a bit of inconvenience in the household."

"Hmm." Simone was thoughtful. "You make a good point, *amour*. But there are practicalities to be addressed. The brute must be bathed after a day on the streets, not to mention fed and watered, as well as regularly taken outside. The chores related to an animal that size cannot be added to anyone already here. The brute must have his own maid. So naturally, Zoe found a street urchin to fill the position."

Hugh threw back the last of his port. "It's unconventional. But a dog such as that may fit perfectly with an urchin. They both come from the street. And the lass is small, but she has a fierceness that is not."

Simone nodded reluctantly. "Perhaps you are right."

"What?" Hugh held the back of his hand to his wife's head. "Are you feeling well? Does a fever ail you?"

"What are you talking about?" Simone batted his hand away.

"You just admitted I was right! I can only assume you're deathly ill!"

"Oh my—you are the most ridiculous man..." She resettled herself with dignity. "You may be right about this, but rest assured, there is still much you are wrong about. I would be happy to provide you with a list."

He grinned. "Of course, my dear."

Chapter Twenty-Nine

Going through Abigail's things felt like a violation. In all the time they'd known each other, their relationship was always tied to the theater. Her rooms at the boarding house were her own. But Rory had convinced Quinton that it was his relationship with her that meant he should do it. He would respect Abigail—her memory and her personal effects. She would want him to do it more than a stranger. So here he was, although he hadn't been able to bring himself to go until the light of the sun shone brightly the next day.

Abigail's boarding house was near the theater, where generations of aspiring actresses had lived before. She started out with her mother in a tiny room on the third floor, with a single window to let in fresh air. But with Abigail's success she now had occupied half of the first floor, with a housekeeper who shared the other half, and meals twice a day if she was around. Abigail led—had led—a comfortable life. She'd done well for herself.

The matron offered little resistance when he asked to see Abigail's rooms. There was little reason to guard a dead woman's home, so she just him showed him in.

Abigail's rooms were tasteful and welcoming. Yellows and purples accented the warm beige walls and ornate furniture, making the overall appearance feminine without being overpowering. The scent of jasmine still faintly hovered in the air, and Quinton breathed in deeply. That was her scent.

The bloodstains that marked where her life had ended were in the parlor. Quinton deliberately didn't look at them.

Instead, he made his way into her bedroom. He noticed a small burst of color near her bed. It was a scruffy figure of a person, made from the scraps of fabric that fell as his mother sewed costumes while he and Abigail played at her feet. He had one as well, though he did not display it. Together they'd had a multitude of adventures with the two figures.

Losing someone who shared so many of his years was immense. Quinton wiped away a single tear; he didn't have time for sentiment. He slipped the toy into his pocket, took another deep breath of jasmine, and got to work.

"What secrets were you keeping, Abigail?" he whispered.

The still air made no reply.

It was near the end of his search that he finally looked in the parlor. Quinton took a poker and stirred the ashes of the fireplace. His efforts were rewarded when a small piece of paper surfaced. He snatched it from the ashes and continued stirring, revealing a second scrap of paper. Despite his attempts, the two scraps were the only treasures yielded by the ash.

Carefully, Quinton wiped the residue away from his prizes.

Came all the way from Irela read one scrap. The other held the words *have agreed to meet him but am afr*.

The handwriting was not Abigail's. Quinton tucked the scraps between the pages of her favorite book—a collection of love poems—and taking his mementos, he took his leave.

He'd found memories and keepsakes, but the charred scraps of burnt paper were the only thing that might prove useful in his investigation.

Chapter Thirty

Sometimes sketching was a form of meditation for Zoe—just emptying the mind and moving the charcoal until a form took shape on the white paper. She didn't really think about whose form it was while she was drawing; she just let her mind go empty and her hand move.

Zoe had lots of portraits of her *mama* and *papa*, as well as her stepfather and her siblings. She would sketch anyone who had an interesting face. Lately it was Mr. Quinton Huxley's face that seemed to dominate her sketchbook. But not today. Today, someone else's face dominated her thoughts.

The events of the previous evening

weighed heavily on her mind. The sight of the red hair with the white streak...she knew it meant something important.

Mary and she had discussed it after they got home, but Mary thought they should wait to contact Quinton. There was nothing to be done so late, and a good nights sleep was always fortifying. At least it usually was—in this case, Zoe wasn't sure she'd slept at all.

As soon as light shined through the window, she sent a boot boy out with a message for Quinton. She'd heard nothing back yet.

Waiting on the reply, Zoe had gone stir crazy in the house. She needed to do something. She usually liked to go to Hyde Park, to draw and paint, but she couldn't risk missing a reply from Quinton this time. So instead she was out in the garden, with the children and the dog, sketching away midst the chaos.

The dog was up and about much sooner than Zoe expected. Rory had bandaged the leg so it wouldn't move at all, but the brute still hobbled about. At first, she tried to contain it, but eventually it became apparent that the effort was futile.

They'd all been calling him "the brute," which led to the natural evolution of Gwen calling him Brutus, and that seemed to have stuck.

For having lived such a violent life, Brutus was surprisingly gentle with the children. He loved Zoe the most, though, and wanted to be near her. Walter and Phoebe took to him immediately. Gwen was just their age, so she fit in well. The four of them were often playing together. It drove the governess mad, but even Simone had softened when it came to Gwen. She had even taken to Brutus, to a small degree.

It was hard not to like the little girl. She was chipper and hard working. Underneath the grime of the street, she was actually a pretty little thing. Her eyes were still bright and hazel colored and her skin color was just dark enough for her heritage to be ambiguous. Her hair was a dark color and came all the way past her waist. Phoebe liked to braid it into all sorts of bizarre styles, but Gwen didn't seem to mind.

When her hand finally stilled, it wasn't Quinton's face looking back at her, or even Mary's or one of the children. It was Lord Driscoll, with his distinctive features, a distinctive streak in his hair. Zoe set her pencil down with a shaking hand.

"Zoe, I'm hungry!" shouted Phoebe.

"Well then go inside and see if Mrs. Bell has some biscuits."

"I don't want to go alone," she pouted.

Zoe sighed. "Fine, let's all go inside."

She began packing up her supplies. Suddenly Mary appeared, and behind her was Ezra. He was still thin and dirty, but at least he had a coat. And his clothes seemed less threadbare. She supposed only having to provide for one person made the odds better for a someone living on the streets.

"Gwen," she called. "Your brother's here."

As he walked past, he glanced at her sketch. His face paled as he grunted and pointed at the face.

"What is it?" Zoe asked.

Of course she couldn't understand him, but that didn't stop him from trying to convey his meaning. Ezra pointed again and gestured something. Zoe threw her hands up, just as frustrated as he was at the inability for them to communicate.

"He says he's seen that man before," Gwen interpreted as she walked up.

"Oh, thank god you're here." Zoe looked directly at the boy. "Where did you see him?"

He gestured again and Gwen said, "He says he saw him the night that carriage came down our street and tossed the girl out."

Zoe's breath caught in her throat. "What do you mean? I thought Quinton asked you about that?"

"Quinton did ask me. He never talked to Ezra."

Looking directly at Ezra, Zoe pointed to the sketch.

"He was in the street?" Ezra gestured. A moment later Gwen answered.

"No. He was in the carriage."

While Zoe blinked rapidly, processing this information, Gwen came around her brother to look at the sketch in question.

"I've seen that man, too." She stepped back and faced Ezra so he could watch her speak. "He looks like the man who saved me from the carriage that day."

Mary tapped the sketch at the hairline. "Did he have this white streak?"

The children discussed it, and Gwen answered. "He had a hat on when I saw him, and Ezra couldn't tell in the dark."

It didn't really matter. The pieces were falling into place. Her eyes met Mary's, and she knew they both were thinking the same thing.

"We can't wait any longer—we need to find Quinton," said Mary.

Zoe nodded. "Gwen, get the footmen to help you load Brutus in the coach. We're leaving, and you and your bother are coming with us."

Chapter Thirty-One

It was late in the afternoon when Quinton finally came home, his grief as heavy as a wet wool coat with stones in the pockets. All he wanted was to open a bottle and find some kind of oblivion at the bottom.

As out of it as he was, it still gave him pause when he heard voices on the other side of his door—inside his home. He always locked the door when he left. Quinton opened it slowly, unsure what to expect.

Mary, Zoe, and the urchins all gathered by the fireplace. The great beast of a dog was there too, his tongue lolling out of his mouth. Quinton noted Oscar's corresponding absence.

Someone had built the fire and made tea, and apparently sweets had been purchased from the bakery two doors down. The remnants of a meat pie or two littered the floor. The group stopped talking as he came in, but before he could say a word, Mary spoke, holding up two hairpins.

"Learned a fair amount from John growing up. How to pick a lock comes in handy from time to time."

Quinton removed his coat and hung it on the peg near the door and rubbed his head. He wasn't in the mood for the chaos this little tribe would undoubtedly bring. All he wanted to do was rage and yell and tell them to get out, but in truth, he didn't have the energy.

As he moved to the fire, a saucer of tea was placed in his hand and a generous amount of whiskey was sloshed into the cup. Zoe placed the bottle within reach. Quinton leaned back with a heavy sigh, but instead of adding to his fatigue, a strange feeling of contentment came over him. He looked out at the group of eyes watching him, feeling the eager energy they were barely holding back.

"Out with it then. I suspect you could have made tea at your place, Miss Demas."

Zoe practically vibrated with excitement. "Thanks to Ezra and Gwen, we have made genuine progress in Lucy's case."

She told him about the urchin's sightings of the Irishman, as well as the similarities between Simon and Lord Driscoll, with liberal help from both Mary and Gwen and several animated bursts of gestures from Ezra. Thus the telling took far longer than it should have, with several convoluted forays into completely unrelated sidebars, and one near come to blows between Gwen and Ezra, but eventually, the story was told.

Quinton was quick to zero in on the gentleman's country of origin. "So the Irishman is our common link. He came into my day as well."

"How so?" Zoe's brow furrowed.

There was no easy way to say the words, so Quinton just said them. "Abigail was killed yesterday."

In the shocked silence that followed, Quinton composed his thoughts. He told the group the facts, ending with his discovery in the ashes. As he pulled out the book of poems from his pocket to show them, the fabric scrap toy was pulled out with it, falling to the floor with a slow flutter. He stared at it for several seconds before picking it up and placing it back in his pocket.

He took the scraps out and laid them out on the footstool, where they were eyed with interest. "Factoring in what you've learned, we have to assume the letter is from Lucy and that Abigail didn't receive it until yesterday. Perhaps Lucy posted it just before she died, as some sort of insurance policy. Whatever was in the letter was enough to lead Lucy's killer to Abigail, and force him to kill again."

"I'm sorry, Quinton. I know you and Abigail were...close." Zoe spoke with sincerity, but he heard the implication.

Quinton shook his head. "It wasn't like that. We grew up together. She was like a sister to me."

The room was silent, the group waiting for him to elaborate. So he did.

"Abigail's mother and my mother were both actresses. They were friends, and having us kids so close in age made them closer. They would help each other out, watching us when one had to be on stage or rehearsing. I remember mother sewing stage curtains, with Abigail and I sitting on the floor working on our letters. Mama would teach us nearly every day, saying we needed to know how to read and write if we were ever going to be anybody."

No one said anything, so Quinton lowered his hand to stroke the dog's head and continued. "Reading came easy to me, but with Abigail, it was different. She got it enough to make her way, but as she grew older schooling wasn't going to be her way up anyway. With her, it would be her looks. She wasn't ten yet when it became obvious she was going to be beautiful, more beautiful than her own mother, or even mine. So her mama got her into acting—taught her the way to imitate accents, how to carry a tune across an audience, and eventually how to socialize with the patrons. After a certain point, she was a shooting star. Nothing could hold her back."

He sighed. "When my mother died, her mother tried to step in, but Abigail and I were too old to share a room anymore, and it was hard enough to feed the two of them without another mouth. I started finding the streets, and that's when I found Charlie and John. But we stayed in touch. She was...special."

Mary laid a gentle hand on his forearm.

"She was a part of the fabric of your life—a part of the tapestry that makes you...you. Beyond all reasonin' or logic, the threads of the tapestries of all our lives are entwinin'. Zoe's maid, the children's lives, your friend—even me. It's become part of the same piece of cloth. I know it's not the same, but your loss is our loss too."

Quinton thought on her surprisingly poetic words. Their lives were entwined now, for better or for worse. Somehow, inexplicably, this strange menagerie had become his tribe. For now, he reminded himself. But he felt the camaraderie and it comforted him.

He shook off his mood, speaking lightly. "Don't get too philosophical on us, Mary. Let's think on this case, and the connections there. I will find time to properly mourn Abigail when this killer is caught."

Mary eyed him shrewdly, but nodded. "We're all thinking the same thing right? Lord Driscoll must've fathered Simon. And we know he dumped Lucy's body. But why? Why would he kill the mother of his child?"

Silence filled the room for a moment, and Quinton spoke next.

"The letter makes it clear that she was

afraid of the Irishman. For lords like him, bairns born on the wrong side of the blanket are just a fact of life. Most just discard them and the mothers. But if she was threatening to expose him, that may be a motive. Or perhaps he took more of an interest in his progeny than most. Maybe he was angry that she took his son across the sea. I don't know. We'll have to ask him."

"Do we think she did take the bairn 'cross the sea?" interjected Gwen. "You never said she were Irish herself."

"She must have been, though she had no accent." Zoe shrugged. "The Driscoll's haven't stepped foot into England for a hundred years."

"Abigail likely taught her to disguise it." Quinton shifted and cleared his throat. "She was quite talented at it."

"Of course. Lucy always did have impeccable enunciation." Zoe leaned forward. "I have no doubt Lord Driscoll is our killer, whatever the motive. Should we contact John?"

"Not yet." Quinton shook his head. "I agree there is evidence, but I don't think it's enough to convict in court. And even if it was, he is, as they say, a toff. Even an Irish toff is above the law, as far as I can see.

"The law." Zoe looked animated. "The law. We need to know the law. We should talk to my father."

Mary shook her head sagely. "I hate to say I told you so, but I did tell you so. Evil travels with that man."

Chapter Thirty-Two

Zoe knew her stepfather would be in his study, even at this late hour. He was like this when he had a thorny case; sequestered as much as possible for weeks, studying precedent and nuance. The trial was in two days' time for this one, so she knew he was in his last-minute panic mode.

She wasn't as sure how he would react to the three of them asking for advice, but she'd convinced Quinton that he would be welcome. She could only hope that was true.

Her stepfather's face registered surprise as she entered the study, followed by both Quinton and Mary. To his credit, he held his tongue, waiting for Zoe to speak.

"I'm sorry for the intrusion, Father. I would not have interrupted if this matter wasn't of the utmost importance." She glanced back at her Quinton and Mary. "We need your advice on a legal matter."

Hugh continued to hold his tongue, assessing the small group. Finally he rose from behind his desk and walked over to Quinton. His face remained stoic, but Zoe knew him well enough by now to recognize the uncertainty on Quinton's face. Hugh stopped in front of him, hesitated, then held out his hand.

"Hugh Dovefield."

Quinton responded immediately with a firm grip. "Quinton Huxley, sir. Thank you for speaking with us at such a late hour."

"Hmm." Hugh caught Zoe's eye, his expression unreadable. "Shall we collect by the fire as I find a bottle of single malt?"

It was only after coats had been hung, chairs had been pulled up and drinks were in hand that the story was told. Hugh listened intently as Zoe told of Lucy's past, and of the baby. It was Quinton who related the conversations with Abigail, her death, and showed him the scraps of letter. Mary broke in with the description of the Irishman and his presence at key moments, as well as a darkly muttered, "Evil travels with that man."

The telling took the better part of an hour, with Hugh stopping them from time to time to ask for more detail or how one thing connected to another. The glasses were empty, and the fire burned down when their words finally ran dry. Hugh leaned back, taking measure of the three of them.

"First, this is top tier work you've all done. I am ashamed to say I would have let all of this lie and simply buried the girl. I'm proud of you, Zoe, for following through on this." His eyes flicked briefly to Quinton as he continued. "I can't say I agree with every decision you have made, but hiring Mr. Huxley was a good one."

It was a small matter in the larger scheme of things, but his praise pleased Zoe more than she expected. She bit her lip to keep from smiling too wide for the tone of their conversation.

Hugh faced Quinton squarely. "You have excellent investigative skills, and good contacts as an investigator. Most importantly, you've kept my Zoe safe. I know from experience that is no simple task. Thank you."

Quinton cleared his throat, clearly surprised, but nodded.

"So your question at this point is what legal steps can be taken?"

"Yes."

Hugh sucked air through his teeth. "Well, it is difficult in a case such as this. Proving paternity of a child is notoriously hard. Unless the father claims responsibility, almost impossible to prove. A resemblance to the child isn't enough."

"What about a witness identifying him as the man who disposed of the body?"

"That is more substantial. However, you said this boy is deaf?"

A sinking feeling came over Zoe. "Yes."

"That's not ideal. A jury will have a hard time believing him to be a competent witness."

Mary pointed at the scraps of the note. "Lucy's own hand identifies him as someone she was afraid of; that has to count for something."

"She doesn't identify him by name. And beyond that, the coroner already ruled her death an accident. The fact he's titled further complicates prosecution."

"So that's it? There's no way to hold a peer accountable? They can do as they please with impunity?" The bitterness in Quinton's tone echoed the feelings of most of the London lower classes.

Hugh sighed. "Well, you're not entirely wrong. Peers can plead 'privilege of peerage' to many offenses, such as not paying debts. And it's neither fair nor morally right. But that is the law. However, treason and murder do not fall under that purview. So technically it is possible to hold a peer accountable for murder. But it's still very difficult."

"In your time as a solicitor, have you ever tried a peer for murder? And won?" asked Mary.

Zoe answered almost absentmindedly. "Father isn't a solicitor. He is a barrister. A solicitor may speak to the accused and provide legal advice, even draft legal documents such as a will, but they cannot present this in court. They are not allowed to speak to the judge or jury. There is an actual railing, or bar in the courtroom that separates the officials from the public. A barrister presents the case in court and can approach both the judge and jury, or as they say, approach the bar."

Pride beamed in Hugh's face as he continued the explanation. "A solicitor often does the research and administrative part of a case. They may be employed by a barrister. I do employ a man, and he is very helpful in court to sort through my documents and find the one I am currently presenting, and give it to me. But I usually prefer to do the research of each case myself, as it helps to more strongly place in my mind each detail. I also usually meet with the client myself, but only once. It gives me a feel of who I am working for. Other meetings my solicitor handles."

He took his own slow sip and continued. "You can actually thank William Garrow for the concept of an accused person having any right to a defense. When I became a barrister there was no such thing. We were essentially prosecutors only. Barrow was appalled that almost anyone could be arrested, tried for a crime and convicted with very little evidence they were guilty. But the thief taker would be paid upon conviction, so he had no interest in truth. It was not unheard of for the actual guilty party to pay the thief taker, so both parties benefited from their scheme while an innocent man had no one to fight for him. Garrow believed each person, regardless of class, should be considered innocent until proven guilty. He was relentless in his quest to reform the law. Thanks to him, now it is far more common for a barrister to be present in the defense of the accused. Almost all of my work presently is for the defense."

"Whether they can pay or not," Zoe added, giving her stepfather a fond smile.

"Garrow won me over," admitted Hugh. "Innocent until proven guilty, regardless the size of their purse."

Mary spoke, a slight tone of sarcasm present. "Well that is all very fascinating, but returning to the matter at hand...as a *barrister*, have you ever tried a peer for murder?"

"No." Hugh sighed again. "It just isn't done."

No one spoke for several minutes, an air of depression hanging over the group.

Quinton spoke first. "You said it was technically possible to try a peer. What would it take? To bring the Irishman to trial?"

Hugh rubbed his chin thoughtfully. "A confession would work. In the hearing of another peer or two would be perfect, or at least impeccable witnesses."

Zoe sighed. "That is impossible. Why would he confess?"

Quinton stood and paced restlessly, swirling his drink as he walked.

"Two women are dead. Abigail was my friend. Lucy's son will grow up without a mother." He glanced at Hugh. "You said it yourself, sir. People have value. Regardless of their station in life. He cannot be allowed to just walk away after taking their lives."

Hugh leaned back in his chair. "I agree with you. But why would he confess?"

"He's a man."

All eyes turned to stare at Mary.

She shrugged and continued. "He's a man and wants credit for his accomplishments—for someone to tell 'im how clever he is. He doesn't want to get caught, but I'd bet money he's burstin' to brag to someone all about what he did."

Zoe cocked her head, considering what she'd said. "She's not wrong. If we could somehow convince him he's won—that he is safe—then perhaps he will tell us what we need to know."

"Well there is the ball."

Quinton stared at Hugh. "Will Lord Driscoll be there?"

"It's *the* ball of the season. Whatever his true motives were in coming to London, one couldn't pretend to be here for the season and not attend the Devonshire ball."

For the first time in the conversation, Zoe felt a glimmer of hope. "You are right! He has his son with him, looking for a well suited match. Of course he will attend." She turned to Quinton. "We can speak with him there, and if we plan it well, others can be within hearing."

"Hmm." Quinton resumed her seat. "I will have to arrange an invitation. But I have a friend or two in high places I can call upon."

"Our plan must be flawless to work," said Hugh.

Zoe was surprised. "Our plan, Father?"

Hugh smiled. "Well, Zoe, I may not be a peer, but I am an impeccable witness. But most importantly, I must know you are safe. Now that I am privy to your schemes, I must insist on being included."

"Very well, Father. Let's work out the details."

Chapter Thirty-Three

The White Heron, an exclusive gentleman's club, was quiet this time of day. Quinton had arrived early, seeking a restorative whiskey and a moment to collect his thoughts. It seemed he drank more whiskey than water these days, but that wasn't the thought he wanted to dwell on.

Abigail was there, swirling in the smoke on the edge of conscious thought, but he wasn't ready to think about that either. Instead, it was a different woman who took center stage as he leaned back and closed his eyes.

He pictured Zoe sitting in the chair across from him the night before, the shadows dancing across her face in the firelight. She was different, to be sure—different in a dangerous, uncontrollable kind of way, like the fire that illuminated her features. Her presence made him feel warm and safe, but he knew if he got too close...he'd burn.

But as the whiskey warmed its way to his soul, Quinton admitted as much as Zoe drove him to the edge of madness, and as much as he knew the risks, he still looked forward to those moments of connection. He sighed, opening his eyes. His entire world seemed to be turned upside down these days.

It didn't really matter. The whole thing would be over soon enough, and his life would go back to the way it was before...more or less. Soon this job would be finished and the last payment made, and he and Lady Zoe Demas would part ways. Perhaps he would occasionally hear news of her through John, but he and Zoe would be strangers again. The thought brought him little comfort. Instead it made him more unsettled.

"They let the dirt in with the wind, I see." A voice to his left broke his musings.

Quinton sighed; he was in no mood for this nonsense today. He turned to see two men standing together, pretending to have a private conversation with each other, all while standing close enough and speaking loud enough for Quinton to hear.

"Days past you could count on seeing quality when you came to White's. Now there is no telling how some people get a membership," said one to the other.

He recognized both men. One was Alexander Dovefield, Zoe's arrogant cousin. The other was a second son of an earl, The Honorable Owen Payne. Though he had little honor, he had nothing to do and plenty of money to do it. Both were known as reprobates, spending far too much time gambling, drinking, and letting their father's money speak for them. Quinton had little time for such men.

"Of course maybe if you have somehow won the affection of a rich barrister's daughter, you would find your way into the best of places, worthy or not." Alexander, already well into his cups before having even arrived at the club, waited for a reaction. When Quinton gave him none, he spoke again. "Or maybe the best of beds, worthy or not. The

French don't view that sort of thing as any differently than petting a dog."

The pampered young lord got the reaction he was waiting for, if not the one he'd hoped.

"Say what you will of me," Quinton growled, pinning him by his throat to the wall with one hand. "But speak of the lady again and you will find yourself with a pistol at dawn."

The surprise in Alexander's eyes made it obvious he knew he'd miscalculated. He was used to battling with words, not fists. He swallowed hard, his eyes darting to his friend, who, unfortunately for him, was just as drunk and useless.

Quinton tightened his grip as Alexander's face turned purple. "Do we understand each other?"

"There you are, Huxley!"

The familiar voice broke through the fog of Quinton's single-minded rage. He turned his head to see the Viscount of Blickling, Lord Montgomery Coleville, standing a few steps away from the obvious altercation.

He spoke again as if nothing were amiss.

"Come join me at my table. I've already ordered your refill."

Quinton slowly released his hold from Alexander's throat and backed off. Both Alexander and young Payne stood stock still as Quinton turned and followed the lord.

As much as Alexander knew he'd miscalculated, Quinton knew he had done the same. In a moment of anger, he assaulted a future Baron. Now he had made an enemy out of a man connected to a friend—a client. It was poor judgment.

Lord Coleville stayed silent as they made their way to his table. When they were seated, he murmured. "When emotions trump reason, the results are usually not what was intended."

"You're not wrong, my lord." Quinton had no desire to speak further of the incident, so he changed the subject.

"Thank you for meeting me. I hope it isn't an inconvenience."

"Not at all, Quinton. I was headed here anyway this evening."

In his mid forties, the lord spoke without tension, as a man comfortable with himself and those around him. As the second son of an Earl, he carried himself with the ease of a man who had wanted for nothing. The untimely death of his older brother many years ago put him in line for the title, a fact he accepted with the expected grace.

Quinton took another sip of his whiskey, studying the man sitting across from him. Though his dark hair was graying at the temples, his broad shoulders and trim waist made him look years younger. Lord Coleville had been gracious to him several times in the past, including his membership at this gentleman's club, and the indecently low rent on the building he leased as his office and home. He thought back to what Charlie had said. *A lucky break.* It really was, as the quality of clientele had certainly improved after that.

"How is your family, Lord Coleville?"

His benefactor laughed. "With a wife and four daughters, my family is why I come to the club."

His words were softened by his smile. Quinton knew he was fond of his all-female household. It was unfortunate for his wife, and he had never been blessed with a son as an heir, especially when the title was to pass to him, but like everything else, he seemed to take it in stride.

"But thank you for asking. They are all well. This will be my eldest's first season, so the women have plenty to keep them busy. I try to stay out of the way when it comes to such things."

"Of course. And your father? I understand the Earl's health has declined." In fact Quinton knew the Earl suffered from gout, but it seemed too personal a thing to bring up to his lordship.

"I understand the same. I actually see little of him. My choice and his."

Unsure how to respond to this surprisingly personal revelation, Quinton hesitated.

Fortunately, the Viscount continued without prompting. "No need to look so scandalized, Quinton. It's no secret my father and I don't see eye to eye. Even his friends, if he has any he could call a friend, would say he is a hard man. When I was a boy, I rarely even saw him. It was my brother, ten years my senior, who filled the role a father should. He filled many roles in our family. Without him..."

The thought of John and Charlie came to mind. They were Quinton's brothers in every sense of the word except blood, and if one of them had died when they were children, he would have been devastated. Even now as an adult, having lost someone he considered being a sister, the loss was so painful he couldn't bear to dwell on it for any length of time, less an abyss of grief swallow him.

"Family is complicated," Quinton finally said. "I've had to be creative with that word, as my childhood is more about bonds than blood."

He was surprised at offering such a personal viewpoint into his own life. A week ago, he would never have given so much away. He blamed Zoe for his sudden interest in sharing.

"The blood of the covenant is thicker than the water of the womb."

"What?"

"People think blood is only shared between those related to each other. But my guess is you've shed your fair amount of blood with your own 'brothers.' The bonds forged by that kind of blood...those bonds can be far stronger than the happenstance of birth." Lord Coleville's eyes were unfocused, staring off into the middle distance. "That's not to say the water of the womb counts for nothing."

"Of course." Realizing Lord Coleville must be thinking with regret on his relationship with his father, Quinton changed the subject. "I have a favor to ask of you, my lord. It's regarding a job I'm working, and I am afraid the trail has led me into your sphere. I was hoping for a way to observe discreetly."

Lord Coleville's brow furrowed. " The gentry? Is this matter serious? Or a bit of some young cad sowing his oats?"

He resisted the urge to point out that those left would regard as a very serious matter the sown oats of young cads ruined in their wake. Now was not the time for a dispute on moral grayness.

"It's a murder, my lord. Hugh Dovefield's family has hired me to make inquires." No need to get into too many specifics.

"Dovefield? That man is a conundrum to be sure. He's a brilliant barrister, if a bit lacking in ambition, and a good man. But I've never understood his choice in clients. You'd think he scoured the workhouse personally just to find them all. Then there's his choice of wife, of course. What possessed him to marry a French woman with a daughter in tow will never make sense to me."

Quinton held his tongue on this matter too. He couldn't afford to alienate Coleville, even though at the moment he thought he was being a real horse's arse.

The Viscount was still talking. "I make a point of knowing who's who in London. Not only who's who but who is under who's skirts, and who is warming who's bed. My father prefers to spend his time at his country estate and out of the clatter of London, but when it's my turn, I will play things differently. I will know who's an ally and who's an enemy, and that will be my advantage."

A sense of unease came over Quinton. He hadn't seen this calculating side of Lord Coleville before. He'd always been more than fair with him, but Quinton wondered for the first time if there was a future cost to his generosity. Charlie always told him he was too trusting by half.

"I will say this, though. Though his moral judgments confound me, I know Dovefield isn't an enemy. If he's hired you to do a job, I'm willing to help. What do you need?"

Quinton dismissed his uneasy thoughts

for the time being. The future would take care of itself. His concern was for the present. He had a ball to prepare for.

Chapter Thirty-Four

Zoe smoothed the light muslin fabric of her outer layer. The fabric was so light it was practically sheer. She wore it over a pastel blue gown, hinting color while still maintaining the luxury of the white muslin. She'd heard stories of certain women of the *ton* wearing nothing at all under the sheer outer layer, but even Zoe wasn't so bold.

Her mother had ordered the gown, especially for this occasion. The Devonshire ball was one of the highlights of the season, and she still hoped that Zoe would catch the eye of some impoverished gentleman desperate enough to court a French aristocrat whose only redeeming feature was a rich stepfather.

She had to admit it flattered her. The soft, thin fabric hung from the empire waist in just the right way to accentuate what curves she had, while the neckline was cut low in a square shape that still left some to the imagination. In a gown like this, Zoe felt ethereal and beautiful instead of like an awkward giraffe. Even better, Mary had done her curls up in a way that made them look soft and elegant instead of wild and unruly. Two spirals hung on either side of her face, framing it perfectly.

Simone had commented that she looked lovely that night—she asked if there was a reason she'd made a special effort. Of course, Zoe had denied such an accusation, but she'd looked at the door six times since arriving.

She tried to pay attention to the girl who was speaking in the small circle of ladies that she'd infiltrated. Mabel Anderson was in her second season, and while she wasn't the loveliest or smartest girl in the bunch, she was adequate in that she came from a well-respected family and had a sizable enough dowry to have a few gentlemen circling. The rumor circulating was that she'd turned down an earl last season because her parents thought she pulled the only eligible duke in the mix. Unfortunately for her, the duke had chosen someone else and Mabel was left with egg on her face. Now she might have to settle for a second son, although you wouldn't know it to hear her tell it. To make matters worse, this was her younger, much more beautiful sister's first season.

"I cannot believe her," said Mabel, batting her big hazel eyes. "She's gone too far this time."

Zoe blinked. "What was that?

"My sister, Margot. Weren't you listening at all, Zoe?"

"Of course I was," Zoe lied. Mabel was always complaining about her sister.

Mabel was still expounding in a condescending tone. "I was saying that she's intent on ruining my life. She chose today, of all days, to disappear. My parents didn't even want to come to the ball; I had to beg them."

Zoe frowned. "What do you mean she disappeared? Aren't you worried?"

"No, of course not." Mabel waved a dismissive hand. "She and father got into some dreadful fight and she left in a huff. I'm sure she'll be back tomorrow, apologetic and batting her eyelashes and all will be forgiven." A serious expression came over her face. "Don't tell anyone though. I don't want any scandal to rub off on me."

"I wouldn't dare." Of course the thing she was most worried about was her own reputation, even though she couldn't resist sharing the drama. "But how do you know she just ran off?"

Mabel blinked. "What else could've happened?"

Zoe opened her mouth, but then abruptly snapped it shut again. It wasn't their fault they were so sheltered. These girls' entire identities were wrapped up in the seasons—until an acceptable man chose them and they were settled, they were just waiting for their place and status in society to be cemented. Any mistake or minor scandal could derail a lady's entire future. The stress of it affected even Zoe, and she did her best to ignore the expectations to society as much as possible.

"Of course, I don't know what I was thinking," said Zoe with a pleasant smile.

Just then, a gentleman came up to ask Mabel to dance, and Zoe could break away. These events always took a toll on her and she could feel the exhaustion wearing her down, even though her family hadn't arrived more than an hour ago.

Her mother and Hugh were across the room making pleasant small talk with his older brother, Lord Baldwin Dovefield, the Baron of Newark, and his much younger wife, Matilda. If ever there was a bigger bore than Baldwin Dovefield, Zoe hadn't met them. He'd never taken to her, and she'd never taken to him.

She knew Alexander had to be around there somewhere, but she hadn't seen him yet and for that she was grateful. He would no doubt track her down at some point in the evening to make a few snide comments—nothing seemed to amuse him more. Zoe tried not to let it bother her, but she also avoided him. She prided herself on a thick skin, but it got old constantly being reminded that she wasn't really a part of the family.

Even after all these years, she didn't have any real friends in the room. There were people she was friendly with, like Mabel, but no one she was truly friends with. Zoe scanned the sea of faces, searching for anyone with whom she could make mindless small talk. Then she saw him.

He entered the room with Lord Coleville. The lord's wife and oldest daughter had arrived earlier. Zoe remembered meeting the girl at her aunt's dinner party, but she couldn't quite remember the name. She thought it might start with an A. The real question was how Quinton knew Lord Coleville, Viscount of Blickling, and future Earl of Kenwood.

While he glanced around the room for a moment, Zoe took the time to examine him. Quinton looked...surprisingly not that out of place. He was in white tie, and Zoe noted the excellent fit of his coat tails. His hair was neatly done and his face clean shaven. If she didn't know better, she might've thought he was just one of the gentlemen.

She found her gaze drawn to the lines of his face. His chin was firm and his mouth set in a firm line. But his best feature was his eyes, dark in this light but with flecks of gold in the sunlight. There was something about him that was drawing, almost magnetic. Zoe cleared her throat, dismissing her thoughts. The fact he was handsome wasn't relevant to their mission.

She wasn't the only one to note his arrival. Any eligible bachelor was noteworthy, but one who was handsome and tall and not yet known? That was blood in the water and the sharks knew it.

It didn't take her long to cross the ballroom; Zoe moved at a quick pace to beat the other ladies there. When he saw her approaching, his lips turned up in a warm smile. She tried to ignore the flutter in her stomach.

"Lady Demas," Quinton said, still smiling.

"Mr. Huxley. I see you did indeed find an invitation."

"Indeed I did."

"You'll have to tell me how you know Lord Coleville sometime."

Quinton shrugged. "It's not that interesting of a story. When I was first starting out, one of my first cases was for Lord Coleville. It wasn't very serious, but he was quite appreciative. We've been on friendly terms ever since. I still lease my office from him."

"Huh. That's very progressive of him."

"He's a good man—for a lord."

"I guess so." Zoe cleared her throat.

People were perceiving their conversation, including her mother. She could feel her appraising eyes taking the situation in, and she suddenly felt incredibly self-conscious.

Quinton seemed to sense her uneasiness. "Would you care to dance?"

Zoe pretended to consult her empty dance card. "Well, I suppose I can squeeze you in."

He took her gloved hand in his and led her on to the floor. The orchestra was just starting a waltz and Quinton moved into it seamlessly, pulling her along with him. She was acutely aware of how close his body was to hers.

Zoe gripped his shoulder tightly. "Where did you learn to dance?"

"My mother." He chuckled softly. "In case I ever met the queen she told me. She taught me the ways of my betters, as if I would someday need those skills. How to talk, how to dance, which fork to use. To her credit, I have managed to put some of those skills to good use."

"Well she was an excellent teacher."

Quinton said nothing, just inclined his head. Even as they conversed, his eyes scanned the room.

"Do you see him?"

"No. Not yet."

"What if he doesn't come?"

"He'll be here."

His words were confident, but Zoe felt his hand tighten around hers. If their quarry didn't show, then she didn't know what they would do. They had to talk to Lord Driscoll without tipping their hand, and this was their best chance to do that.

Suddenly she spotted the flash of red hair streaked with white through the crowd. The Marquess of Kildare had arrived. She could see him standing at the entrance. Brian was also there, wearing a bored expression.

"He's here."

"I told you so." Quinton released his hold on her as the music ended. "Thank you, Lady Demas, for the dance."

"Of course, Mr. Huxley."

They parted ways, but each knew where the other would be headed. Zoe had once heard a safari guide from Africa describe how the lions there would hunt together—separate, but coordinated, moving in unison toward a common goal. That's how she felt in that moment as they moved in on their prey.

She reached him first, as they'd agreed. "Lord Driscoll. How lovely to see you here."

"Ah, Lady Demas. You are a sight for sore eyes, if you don't mind me being too forward." His blue eyes twinkled, as if he was just delivering a clever compliment.

Zoe smiled as if he was the cleverest man at the party. "You certainly are very cheeky, but I'll allow it because you are so charming."

"Ah, you are sweet, dear."

Bile in her throat; she swallowed hard. "It is awfully crowded in here. Have you ever seen the west wing? They have a lovely art collection; even a few by Charles Jervas that might interest you."

"Is that an invitation, lass? A lord and lady, together without a chaperon—how scandalous."

"Perhaps. But it's hardly scandalous; there's servants crawling all over this house."

"Well lead the way then."

He followed her through the crowd. Zoe glanced around for her parents and was relieved to see her mother deep in conversation with Theo, for once oblivious to her actions. She caught her eye as she looked, and the old lady had the audacity to wink.

Hugh was nowhere to be seen. Which meant he was already in place—the lion lying in wait in the grass, waiting for the others to drive the gazelle toward it for the kill.

In her search of the room, she finally spotted Alexander. He was already around the bend with drink, laughing too loud and off balance. He was leaning heavily on Brian's arm. The young man grimaced in embarrassment and gingerly stepped away, leaving Alexander to sway uncertainly. Seeing her watching, the younger Driscoll's wince faded, and he gave her an amiable smile and a shrug. She was struck by how much he looked like his father; in twenty years' time, she imagined it would be like looking into a mirror.

A pang of guilt twisted in Zoe like a knife. He would not smile so easily at her if he knew what she was planning for his father. But justice had to be served, and there was no way to shield the innocent from its effects.

She put thoughts of Brian Driscoll from her mind and focused on the task at hand. They slipped out of the ballroom easily enough, making their way toward the wing she had in mind. Zoe had been to the Devonshire's home many times over the years and she navigated the layout with ease.

Her skin crawled thinking about who was walking next to her, knowing who this man was and what he had done to Lucy. The only reason she could force herself to be this close to him was because Zoe knew Quinton was following close behind.

She stopped in front of a painting. It was one of her favorites. It didn't have a famous artist's name on it. As far as Zoe knew, the name of its creator was lost in time, but she'd always thought it was beautiful.

The painting was of a girl by the seaside. She was young, still at an age of innocence. Her dark hair was unkempt, waving in the wind. She was walking toward the sea, but her face looked back with a questioning expression, as if asking if the viewer was following.

"What a lovely scene," said Driscoll. "Who's the artist?"

"I don't know."

Zoe didn't need to look to feel his presence as he entered the room. She could feel the air shift as Quinton moved to stand on the other side of Driscoll. She let out a slow breath and felt some of the tension ease from her shoulders.

"I think it's about time we had a chat." The words Quinton spoke could've been taken as friendly, but his tone was anything but friendly.

Driscoll didn't seem perturbed. He smiled, as if he'd been anticipating this conversation all along. Zoe's jaw clenched, but she held her tongue. They needed him to feel relaxed and like he was in control, so he would tell them what they needed to know.

"Absolutely." Driscoll lowered himself into a chair and gestured for them to do the same, as if this whole thing had been at his invitation. "I couldn't agree more."

They both followed suit. Zoe opened her mouth to speak, but closed it as a dutiful servant entered the room, offering glasses of claret on a tray. All three took one in silence—after all, it was going to be a long night.

Driscoll waited until the interloper had left the room before downing his in one gulp. "I'm glad you arranged to have this little discussion. I think we all know what this is about, don't we? It's about time we set aside English propriety and spoke plainly."

Chapter Thirty-Five

"Very well, my lord." Quinton leaned back in his chair, his face passive as stone. "You were seen the night Lucy Sherman died, tossing her corpse from a carriage." He took a sip of claret. "Is that plain enough for you, my lord?"

The silence in the room following Quinton's statement hung so heavy that it seemed the air had been sucked from the space. Zoe wondered if the two men could hear her heart beating.

"I don't know who told you that, but I did no such thing." Driscoll's voice was strained. At least they had finally succeeded to throwing him off balance.

"You deny disposing of her body, but you don't deny you knew the girl?"

There was only a moment of hesitation. "No, I don't deny knowing her."

Zoe and Quinton exchanged a glance. They hadn't expected him to admit it so easily. Perhaps this wouldn't be as difficult as they'd thought.

"Were you the father of her child?" asked Zoe, pushing their luck.

"No!" Driscoll shifted uncomfortably. "That's a disgusting accusation."

She knew that was a lie. "Then what was your relationship with her? There's not many reasons for a maid to be known to a nobleman, much less for that nobleman to pursue her across the sea."

Driscoll sighed. "She was...my daughter."

It was Zoe and Quinton's turn to be stunned. Her stomach suddenly turned queasy. If Lucy was running, not from a lover, but from her own father...that somehow made it so much worse.

"I assume not one by your legal wife?" The unsavory thought must've occurred to Quinton as well because his tone had shifted from unfriendly to cold as ice.

"No. Lucy's mother was not my wife's child."

The poor girl. Zoe felt deep sorrow for her.

"Half the gentry has a few offshoots born on the wrong side of the bed. Why should you care about this girl, much less pursue her all the way to London, just because you bedded her mother?"

Driscoll's jawline tightened. "You may not respect me, but you will respect my daughter's memory, Mr. Huxley."

"Please. If you respected your daughter, you wouldn't have bashed her skull in."

"Stop it!" Driscoll stood, emotion finally overtaking him. He took a deep breath, steadying himself. "I have no idea why my Lucy is dead. The only thing I do know with certainty is that I did not harm her."

Zoe eyed him thoughtfully. His impassioned speech sounded genuine. But appearances could be deceiving. And she knew from Lucy's own hands she feared this man—her father.

She tried a different approach. "Who was Lucy's mother?"

Driscoll's brow furrowed at the change of

subject, but he answered. "She was the widow of one of my tenant farmers. Her husband died in a terrible accident—I felt obligated to go and see her; to assure her that the tenancy was still hers if she wanted to stay. My own life was...troubled. My wife was ill and my son and I were not on very good terms. I was lonely and she was lonely. One visit turned into another and then another and another, until there was a consequence that couldn't be undone."

Quinton's lip curled in disdain. "Charming."

"I'm not proud of what I did. There's no excuse for it. But Lucy was innocent in all of it."

Zoe didn't comment on the morality. "And you maintained a relationship with her? I imagine that was awkward at home."

"The timing was such that she could pass Lucy off as her husband's. For a time I kept my distance, only visiting on birthdays or Christmas. But then the flu took both my wife and Lucy's mother within a week of each other. The loss was too much—I couldn't abandon her after that. I took her into my home. Her presence eased my suffering and grief, but I'm afraid it made my son's worse."

"So he knew she was his sister." Zoe frowned. Brian hadn't mentioned that—of course it wasn't something one brought up to a casual acquiescence. But nothing in his tone or body language had indicated even a remote familiarity with Lucy.

"We didn't discuss it at first, but he knew. Brian was many things, but he wasn't a fool. He could never forgive me for it. I was trying to do the honorable thing by my daughter, but it seemed anything I did to help one hurt the other. There was an incident when Lucy fell and broke her arm. At least that is what she told me. The way she looked at him after that, it just made me wonder. When the situation finally became untenable, I sent him to a boarding school. I thought maybe some distance would help—perhaps temper off some of the rough edges."

"And did it?"

Driscoll sighed again, rubbing his hands together. "It seemed to help. He would come to visit and he seemed...better. Less angry. We are at least on civil speaking terms. When he came back home for good, I thought he'd finally matured. It seemed like a good start."

A thought had formed in Zoe's mind, and when she looked at Quinton, she could see he was of the same mind.

"When did your son return home permanently?" asked Quinton.

"Well, it would've been about two years ago now. He was done with university, and we agreed his place was on the estate."

Zoe wished she had more wine. "How long after that did Lucy leave?"

"Maybe two months." Driscoll hung his head. "But that's not why she left."

"Why did she leave?"

"She told me some farmer's hand had gotten her in the family way, and I'm afraid I didn't handle the news very well. I was upset and angry. She left that night." Driscoll's voice softened so it could barely be heard. "That was the last time I saw her. I thought she would come back after a few days, but a few days turned into a few weeks and then months and before I knew it more than a year had gone by with no word from her."

Quinton stood suddenly, agitated. "Then why are you here? The girl left and took her problems with her. What did you want from her?"

Driscoll blinked in surprise at the outburst. "She contacted me."

A stunned silence fell over the room, but only for a moment before Driscoll continued. "The bairn was ill and she asked for some money—just a few pounds. I sent the money right away to the address she provided, but when I didn't hear from her again, I decided to come and speak with her in person. The address ended up not belonging to her—it was the flat of some actress or another. She wouldn't tell me anything. I asked her to contact Lucy and tell her I was in town and wanted to talk. But it wasn't hardly 24 hours before I heard my daughter was dead. I'd waited too long and missed my opportunity."

Driscoll's head still hung low, but Zoe could see the tears forming in his eyes. Despite herself, she found she believed him. Besides, whether or not he knew it, his tale presented a new suspect—one she'd never considered before.

"What is it you wanted to discuss?" she asked softly.

"I wanted to make things right."

"How?"

"Before Lucy left, I had already contacted my solicitor to include her in my will. She was to receive half the inheritance, not including the title and entailed property that would go to Brian of course. I wanted to tell her I had also decided to include her child in that inheritance, so that they would be provided for should anything happen to her. I wanted her to know that I had accepted them. I wanted her and the bairn to come home."

Zoe rose quickly and reached out to grab Quinton's arm on instinct, all sense of propriety lost in the moment's urgency. She didn't have to say it; he had also come to the same conclusion. They rushed out of the room, nearly colliding with Hugh, who was listening in at the door.

"Have you seen Brain Driscoll?" The question came out breathless, as if she'd been running upstairs.

He shook his head silently, and the trio rushed back to the ballroom, the confused older Driscoll following in their wake.

"Wait," he said. "I just want to know if you know the location of my grandchild?"

Zoe didn't respond; the only thing she

could think of was finding the younger Driscoll. When they reentered the ballroom, she glanced about desperately. She didn't see the fiery colored hair, but she spotted Alexander within a few seconds.

She grabbed him by the arm and spun him around. "Where is Brian?"

"What?" His unfocused eyes blinked slowly, his drunkenness slowing his reactions. "Who's Brian?"

Zoe could've screamed with frustration, but she forced herself to speak clearly in only a slightly raised tone. "Brian Driscoll. The man you were speaking with not ten minutes ago? Red hair? Irish accent?"

Comprehension dawned. "Oh, that guy. Yeah, he gave me this note to give to you." Alexander reached into his waistcoat and nearly tipped over. Quinton grabbed his jacket and righted his balance while Zoe ripped the piece of paper out of his hands.

I think we all know the game has come to an end. Come to Hyde Park. Rotten Row. By the meadow. Bring Lucy's bastard, or I'll kill the dummy. A boy for a boy. Only

THE TIES THAT DIVIDE

one of you needs to come, I don't care which. You have one hour.

Chapter Thirty-Six

The frosty night air galvanized the whole party to action as they sent for their respective coaches. Quinton turned to Zoe, his heart pounding in his chest.

"I need to go get Simon."

Zoe sucked in a sharp intake of breath. "You cannot be considering trading him for Ezra."

"Now hold on—" started Lord Driscoll.

"Of course he isn't." Lord Dovefield spoke impatiently. "But we'll never get close enough if we don't bring something to bargain with."

Quinton nodded, grateful for Hugh's quick take on the matter. "I would never trade one life for another. But he is right. We cannot even get close unless he thinks the trade will happen."

"Very well," said Driscoll reluctantly. "But I insist on going with you. He's my grandson, and I'm not letting him out of my sight."

"Fine."

Driscoll stalked down to his carriage, impatient to start the journey.

"We will need authority to arrest him." Hugh looked at Zoe. "Zoe and I will send word to John. Then we'll meet at the park."

"He did say to come alone," Zoe pointed out.

Quinton shook his head. "He may have said that, but he must know his father will come."

"We will keep to the shadows, until the boy is safe and John can make an arrest."

"What in the name of all that is holy is going on out here?" Lady Simone Dovefield stood at the top of the stairs, silhouetted in the light like a terrifying goddess of the night. "I don't know all that is going on, but I demand an explanation."

"Are we in a rush or not?" shouted Driscoll from his carriage.

The group froze for a moment, like mice in front of a cat. Quinton caught Zoe's wide eyes.

"Well, I should be going." He swallowed, avoiding the lady's gaze. "Good luck with...this."

He hurried down the last few steps, leaving father and daughter to deal with the fallout. Quinton climbed onto the driver's box of Driscoll's curricle, waving off his usual driver. He drove recklessly toward Charlie's, desperate to get Simon and meet with Brian—desperate to get Ezra back.

Ezra. The thought of the boy made his blood run cold. As he expertly navigated the narrowing streets approaching Charlie's place, he cursed himself for being an arrogant fool. How ironic that as he thought he was improving Ezra's life, he'd been putting him in the sights of a killer.

∽

Simone took the explanation about as well one would expect—which was to say, poorly.

Zoe and Hugh eventually convinced her to continue her rant in their carriage. Hugh shouted at the driver to take them back to the house.

Zoe interrupted the non-stop lecture. "Father, we don't have time to go home; we need to get word to John. Mother will just have to come with us."

"Oh, well I'm glad you feel—"

"Hyde Park is near enough to the house."

"The meeting place is near the house. We'll send a footman to get John. It'll be the fastest thing." Hugh closed his eyes, rubbing his temples. "We need to go home either way. We can't go without Gwen. She's the only one who can talk to the boy."

"Now wait just a minute. You can't just expose an innocent child—"

"Simone!" Hugh's tone was stern. "You are absolutely correct. There are few good options in the scenario. But I need you to understand that this night is not going to go your way. In tomorrow's light things will be different, but tonight, I need you to trust me."

Zoe waited with bated breath for her mother's reaction. She'd never heard her stepfather speak to her in that tone.

Simone's jaw tightened. "Very well. But we will be having a discussion tomorrow."

"I never doubted it, my dear."

∼

Charlie's residence was all the way on the other side of the city. It was almost an hour later when Quinton and Driscoll returned, having finally reached the meeting spot. Rotten Row was a road, a popular place to ride a horse during daylight hours. This time of night, it was deserted.

A few paces off the road, the full moon cast a bright glow on their villain. Brian Driscoll sat on a bench, with Ezra beside him. In his hand was a dueling pistol, pointed squarely at the boy's temple.

Quinton slowed the carriage, keeping his eyes locked with Ezra's terrified ones, and called out. "I'm here, Driscoll. Let the boy go."

"Do you have the brat?" Brian shouted back. "Bring him out where I can see him!"

The older Driscoll slowly opened the door to the carriage and stepped down. Simon was in his arms, his fat little arms wrapped around his neck. Quinton glanced around nervously; he didn't see them, but he had to assume the Dovefields and John were tucked away somewhere nearby.

"You!" Brian's words were slurred, as if well into his cups. "I said just one of them and the baby! What are you doing here?"

Driscoll didn't answer his son. He just stared at him, with an expression on his face that could only be described as deep, bottomless sorrow.

Quinton stepped down from the driver's seat, moving to stand near Driscoll and Simon. Suddenly the bushes moved and a blur of motion threw itself at Quinton's legs.

"Gwen?" Quinton peeled her away from his body and looked her in the face. "What are you doing here?"

"Who is this?" Brian scoffed. "I tell you to come alone, and you come with a plus two? Is this your first hostage exchange? What's the matter with you?"

Gwen spoke in quiet, hurried gasps. "Lady Zoe and the mister and the runner are in the trees. They're ready when you need them, but I 'ere for Ezra. He got no voice without me."

"Fine, fine." It was a good idea, though Quinton didn't love exposing the girl to danger. "Just stay close to me."

Driscoll addressed his son. "What's the plan, Brian? You must know I won't allow you to murder this child in cold blood…like you did your sister."

"This is your fault. Yours! I am your son." Brian's eyes were crazed. "I deserve the title and I deserve the money! And yet you cared only for your bastard daughter. I knew she was pregnant. Another bastard. I thought you would forget her. I was glad she was leaving. I told her I would kill her child if she ever came back. But you wouldn't let it go and came after her."

"What about Abigail?" If Driscoll was in the mood to monologue, Quinton wanted to know that part of the story too. "She had nothing to do with this."

"That was Lucy's fault too. She sent her that stupid letter. I just wanted to know where he was—where the baby was. But she wouldn't say a word, and she pulled a knife, like I couldn't get past a knife."

"Seems she did get a lick or two in." As he'd been speaking, Quinton had been moving forward. Brian's right forearm glistened in the moonlight. Whatever bandage had been binding the wound until now must've shifted in the struggle.

"If she had told me where the boy was, I would have left her alive. She just wouldn't tell me." His voice rose.

"So you could kill him, too." His father hadn't moved. He was still just standing there, with that sorrowful expression.

Brian continued as if he hadn't heard, his pitch at the point of near sobbing. "Even with her dead, you were going to split the assets with her bastard son. Why not me, Father, why did you never care for me?"

Through the mad ravings, Quinton understood the motive. Why Lucy ran away. Why Lucy was killed. Her own brother, mad with jealousy, wanted his rival gone.

"I loved you both, Brian," replied Driscoll. "She was my daughter. I gave you everything you could want. It was leftovers I had for Lucy. Leftovers. You had the castle and the land. I loved you too, Brian. Always."

"You gave her all your love." In a split second, Brian had become eerily composed. "You did this."

The words held almost no emotion. But with each one, he jabbed the pistol angrily at his father. Quinton knew it was time to act.

"Tell your brother to drop," he said whispered to Gwen.

She immediately gestured to Ezra, whose eyes had been glued to Gwen's. Ezra swung away from Brian, hurling his body to the ground. Quinton moved at the same time, almost upon him when a shot rang out.

Brian's eyes went wide and his left hand let go of the pistol. He reached up to touch the growing red stain on his chest, his fingers coming away stained. He looked with an expression of astonishment, his gaze going over Quinton's shoulder. Then his eyes rolled in the back of his head and his body slumped forward just in time for Quinton to catch him.

Quinton knew that the man's body held no more life. He laid him gently on the ground and looked back.

Driscoll still held the gun pointed straight out, as if frozen. Hugh and John were running toward him. They stopped short as they took in the fallen man, Ezra cradled in Gwen's arms, and the gun in Driscoll's hand. No one could've anticipated this.

After what seemed like an eternity, Driscoll spoke. "He was mad. I should have seen it when he was a boy... there was always something amiss with him. Something broken inside. I was blinded by my own blood. I did nothing, and he killed my Lucy."

He met Quinton's eyes. "He was mad. There was no other choice. He was my responsibility."

John came up beside him. "My lord, give me the pistol, please."

"Oh." Driscoll finally lowered the weapon and placed it into John's waiting grip. "I didn't realize you'd involved a constable."

"Bow Street Officer, sir." John stuck the gun in his pocket. "This is no place for a child, sir. Please, go wait with him in your carriage."

Driscoll nodded absentmindedly, turning his back to the sight of his heir, his only son, lying in a broadening pool of his own blood. Through the whole thing, Simon had not spoken a word.

Quinton stood up slowly, his hands sticky with blood. Suddenly he was aware of Zoe by his side. Hugh and John stood in front of him, and beside Hugh was his wife. That was a surprise.

"He killed his own son."

"We saw. We saw all of it," said Zoe.

Hugh spoke softly. "Impeccable witnesses who need to get their story straight."

Chapter Thirty-Seven

Because of the excitement and very late night, breakfast was closer to luncheon the following day. There was indeed a conversation had around the dining table with Simone, but it wasn't as harsh as Zoe expected.

Considering the wild night, which included an actual shooting and death, the spirit in their home was surprisingly pleasant. It was as if the terrible sight had made them more appreciative of each other. And the experience seemed to have softened Simone.

Simone took a sip of her coffee, a contemplative expression on her face. "I just cannot stop thinking of Lucy, alone with a child, no one to turn to for help. She must have been so terribly frightened. And yet we had no clue."

"It's a sad reality, dear, but there must be hundreds or even thousands of mothers like Lucy out there." Hugh said the sad words with a sigh.

"That doesn't even count orphans, like Ezra and Gwen," said Zoe through a mouthful of custard.

"Where is the brother now? Ezra?"

It was Hugh who answered. "He left with Mr. Huxley. I know nothing more."

Simone remained deep in thought. "Perhaps there's more we could be doing to help with the overall problem. Matilda is always trying to foist those charities at me...perhaps I should take a closer look."

"For now, my dear, let us be content with a positive outcome for Lucy's child."

It was Hugh who had quickly taken charge the night before. The general consensus of those present was that charging Driscoll with his son's murder would accomplish nothing. With the hostage situation, it would be difficult to gain a conviction. Besides which, Brian was a murderer who killed two women. The fact his death had come at his father's hands seemed to be its own type of poetic justice.

And there was the child. To deprive him of the only family he had left seemed cruel in the larger scheme of things.

So Hugh came up with an alternative option, which he offered to his lordship. Leave that night for Ireland. Concoct whatever story he wished as to what happened to Lucy and Brian, or who the child was, but take Simon and leave now. Of course, he took the offer.

Ezra ran to Bow Street for a wagon for the body. John agreed to take responsibility for killing Brian, and Quinton and Hugh would back up the story. (Zoe offered, but they seemed to think men's testimony would be taken more seriously.) He would get a bonus for finding Lucy's killer and being the one to bring him down.

The women were bundled into a carriage and sent home before the cavalry could arrive, leaving the men behind to tell the story to whoever showed up with the wagon. Hugh hadn't arrived home until the light of dawn was peeking over the horizon.

"At least Lucy has justice now," Zoe said softly. "The more I have learned about who she really was, the more I wish I could have known that person. The opportunity is lost, but at least there is justice."

The rest of the meal was eaten in quiet contemplation. Finally Hugh left to attend to his actual responsibilities. Simone looked at her daughter and poured her another cup of coffee.

"I need to change, *mama*. My first resolution is that I want to learn the names of all the staff. It's not much, but it's a start."

Simone smiled. "As angry as I was, I'm also proud of you, *chaton*. I think your resolution is a good one, but you have already changed. You stood your ground, not for yourself, but for someone else. You did it for Lucy."

"I did start the ball rolling," Zoe admitted. "But the people I found along the way are the reason it all came together. And, strangely, I don't feel quite so out of place anymore."

"You have found a *connexion*, people who fit you. It is a *tribu improbable*."

Zoe had to agree. It was an unlikely tribe. She was grateful that her mother did not ask for more details on her feelings for Quinton, though the question hung between them. The conversation would have to be had eventually, but not today.

She smiled at Simone and rose to go. "I have asked Aunt Theo if Mary and I may stay there for a few days. It has been a taxing time for me. Is that all right with you?"

"And your *tribu*? Will they be there as well?"

"I think your tribe always finds you, don't you, *mama*?"

Chapter Thirty-Eight

To Quinton's great surprise, Zoe's Aunt Theo invited the whole tribe over for after dinner drinks that Friday evening. He received an invitation by boot boy, and sent a positive reply with the same boy. It was a surprise, but not an entirely unwelcome one.

When he arrived and was announced, he was pleased to see he was not the first to arrive. John was already there, his comfortable nature making it easy to chat with the Dowager. Instead of his usual Runner's livery, he wore a well fitted suit. While not the latest fashion, John was always at ease in his own skin, which somehow made his clothes fit better.

Mary was there as well, this time not as a maid, but as a guest. Her dark green dress hugged her generous curves, suiting her dark complexion. The dress was stylish in an understated way and fit her perfectly. Knowing the differences in size between her and Zoe, he suspected Mary had sewn the dress herself. She wore her hair in a looser style than was customary, with a wide band of fabric keeping the considerable volume of curls contained. She looked...happy.

Then there was poor Charlie. He was the most out of place, standing awkwardly in a corner. His suspicious nature had kept him alive in more than one instance, and he was loathe to trust surface festivities such as these. Fine whiskey would either help or hinder his mood, and one never knew which. His own dress was casual for the occasion, but certainly a step up from his usual breeches and shirt.

Perhaps Rory was the biggest surprise. He arrived after Quinton, with a suit of the latest cut, his cravat tied in the most fashionable knot. His reddish blond hair was cut precisely, his boots shined to a luster, and his manners impeccable. He greeted the

Dowager with admiration and warmth, his faint Scottish brogue charming as ever. Quinton shook his head at his confounding friend. Did he have an actual valet on hire? Was he himself a valet in a previous life? The contradictions of the Scotsman never ceased.

And then there was Zoe. She was staying with the Dowager for a time, so was present as a secondary hostess to greet each guest as they were announced. Her dress was the pale blue color she favored, the neckline more modest than was fashionable, but certainly enough to not go unnoticed. The cut was becoming, and the color somehow made her already striking eyes seem even bluer. For now the ocean was calm, he thought as he looked into them.

His gaze shifted to the huge dog at her side. "He has found his place?"

Zoe reached down and stroked the dog's soft fur. "Brutus has fit right in. He hardly leaves my side, except to accompany Gwen outside. And my parents are surprisingly agreeable to him."

"They always know who saves 'em," muttered Charlie from his corner.

A drink placed in his hand, Quinton

chatted briefly with the Dowager and soon moved into the sitting area. It was a small space, but small sitting areas lent to more intimate gatherings. By mutual silent accord, all of them found seats.

Quinton nodded at John. "The magistrate buy what you were selling that night?"

"He sure did." John chuckled. "I don't know if he really believed every word, but he does like a nice, neat fix to a rather complicated problem. Having Mr. Dovefield for backup didn't hurt."

"And what of Ezra? How is he faring after such a trauma?" asked Zoe.

"He seems the same. I've been letting him spend the colder nights by my fire, though." The three men shared a glance. "We know a fair bit about the difference a bed by the hearth can make. And Gwen?"

Zoe smiled. "My mother seems to have taken a genuine interest in her. When she is not busy with Brutus, she's teaching her maths and letters. Gwen is a quick study. She'll soon be reading. Her accent is even becoming somewhat understandable."

Mary interjected. "Something's been

bothering me. I can see where Ezra saw the drawing of the father and recognized the son. They did look a great deal alike. But what of the man saving Gwen from the street? Which of them did that?"

"That was the father," John answered. "When your father spoke to him he said he knew the girl, that he had grabbed her just before the wheels of the carriage crushed her. Apparently that was just happenstance."

Charlie spoke next. "What of the mite that stayed with us?"

"He is in Ireland by now. We can only hope the best for the bairn." John frowned. "I am a bit of the feeling that the man who raised a son with the twisted mind of Brian Driscoll might share a bit of the blame for the twisting."

Rory spoke. "Perhaps. But I think some minds are twisted from birth, no blame to anyone. Then the family ties that should bind can become the very ties that divide. Driscoll did right by Lucy at the beginning, and tried to make up for his mistakes in the end. That's all you can ask of any man."

"I knew there was evil with the father." Mary paused to collect her thoughts. "I felt it as sure as I am speaking now. But now I think the evil was with him, not in him. It was the son that evil lived in. The boy will fare well."

John shrugged. "Well, if you say so."

Mary turned to Quinton. "The town has been quite abuzz with the news of Abigail's death. There has been more than one vigil. She was loved by many."

"Yes, they did love her, in their own way. From afar. But she was my sister of sorts, and I will always know who the real Abigail was. They can have their vigils. I will keep my memories."

The chatting continued, leading to smaller groups breaking off into more intimate conversations. Zoe found herself sitting near Quinton.

"This experience was exhilarating, but also... satisfying." She leaned back into the armchair. "I needed to have answers and we found them. Thank you for allowing me to be a part of it. I know I am not always the easiest person to have around."

Quinton smiled. "I rather got used to your ways, milady."

They both paused as Theo's voice rose. She had been debating the merits of several books with Rory. They both agreed the recent anonymous work, *The Woman of Color*, was a literary masterpiece, with Rory showing none of the present English embarrassment for a man to read it. But now they had moved on to less agreement. Although all were aware of Rory's fondness of Shakespeare, he was also willing to make room for the works of Harry Fielding. Known for being the magistrate of London and establishing the Bow Street Runners, Fielding also had a body of literary work of which Rory was a fan. Apparently the Dowager preferred Ann Radcliffe for her supernatural novels, and was willing to describe them with a fair amount of passion.

Eventually they had to agree to disagree. Theo excused herself, moving to sit next to Zoe and Quinton.

She reached out a hand. "May I see that watch you care so much for?"

Quinton stared at her, reluctant to give her what she was asking for. It was the same feeling of dread that had come over him when John came to tell him of Abigail's death. It was the feeling that by giving the watch to the Dowager, something would change—that as long as she didn't say whatever it was she was keeping in aloud, it wasn't real yet.

The silence deepened, but he made no move. He just wanted his world to stay the same.

The Dowager spoke softly. "I think you need to hear what I have to say, my boy. It's just words. You can do with them as you please."

It was the words he feared. Quinton hesitated another long moment, but finally relented and reached into his pocket, drawing out his beloved watch. He had little from his father, but he cherished this.

Theo took it carefully and, as she had before, ran her thumb over the worn crest on the side of the watch. "It's as I thought." She looked up at Quinton. "How much do you remember of your father?"

"Very little. He died when I was quite young. I know my mother loved him deeply."

"I'm just a crippled old lady, my boy, and sometimes time hangs heavy on my hands. So I find things to interest me. People are interesting in how they connect. I have the books of the family lines and the peerage and the crests and..." Theo paused. "I found that crest. It's old and it's changed with the years, with this one marrying that one and all. But if that watch comes from your father, it must have come from his grandfather. Your father was a noble. You were born on the wrong side of the blanket, but a noble nonetheless."

Quinton stared at her for an eternity buried in a moment of time, then stood up abruptly. He held out his hand for the watch.

He spoke quietly while Theo handed him his watch. "Respectfully, Your Grace, I am not naive. My mother was an actress. Actresses don't have husbands, they have patrons. I've never indulged myself in the fantasy my parents were married to each other. But whatever their relationship, I know my mother grieved for him the rest of her life, which was far too short. Her one wish was for me to find someone who loved me as my father had loved her."

The watch placed safely back into its pocket, Quinton continued. "What she did not tell me is my father's family name. There is nothing to be gained from the knowledge, other than resentment on both sides. I would prefer to respect my mother's wishes, and leave the past in the past."

Theo rose as well. "I meant no disrespect, my boy."

"None taken, Your Grace. In fact, I already have a family, cobbled together to be sure, but bound by an unbreakable covenant of blood."

"Very well. If those are your wishes, I will respect them." She looked around the room. "Enough of this. It's a party is it not? Now this old lady needs a bit more refreshment."

As the Dowager moved off, Quinton turned to Zoe. She said nothing, but he saw the clouds in her eyes. Not yet a storm. More like a sky with equal chances of parting for the sun, or gathering for rain.

Neither of them said anything. He turned away, choosing to make his way to John and Charlie, who stood together in deep conversation. He needed his brothers.

He didn't contribute to their conversation, but rather just stood and let their words wash over him. The dowagers' words, promising a revelation of the past, tugged at him, but he put the conversation aside. His life had turned out better than he had any right to expect. He would embrace what he had.

When Charlie excused himself to seek

another drink, John leaned toward Quinton. "Not to change the mood of the evening, but you'll be needing to find me on the morrow. You remember how tightly wound the magistrate was, keeping an eye out for a dead girl? Well, they found 'er, just like the magistrate said—and there is something you need to see."

About the Authors

Sandra and Taylor Preisler share a love of reading and writing, an obsession with foster kittens, and of course DNA. The Ties That Divide is the mother daughter duo's debut novel and somewhat surprisingly, both survived the experience. Most of the time they even enjoyed it. While both are from Casper, Wyoming, Taylor now lives in Phoenix, Arizona with her sister, roommate, two Pit Bull's and probably some of those pesky fosters. Sandra and her husband Ken split their time between beautiful Wyoming and equally beautiful Arizona.

Their two cats love the change every time and have never complained.

◼️f facebook.com/sandraandtaylorpreisler

Also by
Taylor & Sandra Preisler

The Ties That Divide

The Wounds That Linger

Made in United States
North Haven, CT
03 April 2025